Remembering
»–the Way→

Greta Beekhuis

Andrew Benzie Books
Pleasant Hill, California

Published by Andrew Benzie Books
www.andrewbenziebooks.com

Printed in the United States of America

First Edition: August 2016

10 9 8 7 6 5 4 3 2 1

Beekhuis, Greta
Remembering the Way

www.rememberingtheway.com

ISBN: 978-1-941713-39-6

Cover and book design by Andrew Benzie

This book is dedicated to Adele

ACKNOWLEDGEMENTS

I'd like to thank all of the people who helped to birth this book. In particular, I am deeply grateful for the friendships of Adele Ray, Jane and Harry Edelstein, Rachael Herron, Lori Cope, Bruce Aronow, Roger Simon, Ann Miner, Gary Crawford (and his fellow band members of Home By Dark) and Melissa Hardy.

I am pleased to have worked with Andrew Benzie to publish this book.

The encouragement of my family has been crucial for the success of this adventure. My children, Andrea and Joey, are the lights of my life.

I am fortunate beyond measure to share this journey with my beloved traveling companion and partner, Kalle Kanerva.

CHAPTER ONE

Larry switched on the light and sighed contentedly as he surveyed the immaculate lab that was now his own. It felt like the research could finally move forward with the space and resources dedicated to his mission. After years of frustration in academia, battling with administrators who had never even set foot in a lab and had no clue as to how research was really performed, he had found an angel investor who was willing to pull out all the stops. The circumstances that brought them together were still astonishing to Larry. He ran his hand along the smooth edge of his desk and let his mind wander back to the beginning of this adventure...

He had been sitting in a meeting called by the Resources Director; idly scrolling through Twitter under the conference table while the whiteboard filled with strategic analysis buzzwords. His rare disease searches usually produced papers long abandoned by other labs, but this time an advocacy group appeared. "Patient group with investor willing to fund research, eager to meet with scientists" the post read. Larry's heart began to race.

He glanced up at the board and groaned as the Resources Director droned on.

"Let's do another SWOT analysis, team. Strengths, Weaknesses, Opportunities and Threats."

Larry thought, "Oh, Good Lord, such a waste of time!"

Eager postdocs were raising their hands to help the Director fill in the blanks in each quadrant, as he nodded at one of his favorites. "Oh, very good Robert, we'll certainly follow up on that idea."

Larry remembered when he had been that postdoc, drinking the Kool-Aid of the department chairs, working long hours for little pay and no recognition. His tenure had been secured with a steady stream of funding from the National Institutes of Health over two decades of late night grant writing, but that had dried up as the government moved on to data driven projects and left most of the basic researchers in the dust.

He put his phone on the table and it buzzed loudly. "Pardon me, gentlemen, I've got to go see a patient." He'd always wanted to say that, ever since he got his PhD and his title became Doctor.

The Director turned around, red faced. "I'm not FINISHED," he hissed.

"Oh, but I am!" Larry heard himself say, as he quickly left the room. He jogged down the hall and out into the sunshine. It felt like he was finally free after a long jail sentence. He ran to the parking garage, got into his car and sped away. Looking into the rear view mirror, he half expected to see squad cars. What had his life become?

He pulled into the shopping mall parking lot and opened the Twitter feed again on his phone. The tweet was still there. He clicked the icon, followed the account and sent the tweet to himself at his home email. Then he went into the electronics store to buy a new phone.

Larry knew that this would have to be clearly separated from the accounts that the University monitored with their invasive algorithms. He was perfectly aware that by following the account of the patient advocacy group he was exposing himself to censure, but he welcomed the discussions that were surely to come.

He took a number at the customer service kiosk and sat in a chair, letting his mind wander through the possibilities. He would go back to the office tomorrow, of course, and continue his work like a good little soldier, but there was a light at the end of the tunnel now, and he felt certain that there was a way out, a way to remember why he had become a scientist in the first place.

He jumped, a little startled, when his number was called. The new phone was a basic refurbished model, already charged, and with just enough memory to function as a lifeline.

He drove home carefully, marveling at the difference in the traffic at this time of day. Usually he left his desk late at night, just after the janitors finished their rounds in the labs. Now he was in the afternoon sunlight, surrounded by suburban soccer moms and grocery shoppers.

His heart was pounding as he let himself into his house at the end of the block. It looked like all of the other houses on all of the blocks in the neighborhood, perhaps a little more unkempt, but still innocuous.

He usually left his keys on the small table in the front entry, hung up his coat and made his way to the bedroom to get a few hours of sleep before he had to get back to his post in the early morning before the students filled up all of the parking places. Instead of his usual routine, he went into his study, and began unpacking a box that had been sitting next to his desk for weeks. It was his brother's old desktop computer, one that he had given to Larry when he upgraded to the latest model after the most recent merger in his company.

Larry set up the computer and signed in as a guest user. He spent the next few hours researching the patient advocacy group. It was small, but well funded, and they had a few scientific folks on their board of directors, but it looked like they were all members of the same golf and country club.

He went back into the kitchen and opened the refrigerator. It was empty. He had become so accustomed to eating in the University cafeteria that he could not remember the last time he had been to the grocery store or cooked himself a meal.

The kitchen was covered in a fine layer of dust. Larry opened the cabinet under the sink and took out some cleaning supplies. He made a passable attempt at sanitizing the surfaces and then went back to his study. He wasn't really hungry, but decided perhaps he'd do something he hadn't done since, since when exactly, he couldn't actually remember. He got back in his car and went out to eat.

While he waited for his grilled salmon and salad, he pulled out the new phone and did some more searching on social media. He found the photos of the patient families gathered at a picnic fundraiser at the golf and country club. It was a small group, but still, these were actual patients! Larry felt so hopeful that he generously tipped the waiter, and walked out of the restaurant, humming. It felt like decades of weight was falling off of his shoulders.

He had been feeling as if his life's work amounted to nothing other than a small book in the University library, published so long ago that he doubted anybody had ever checked it out. He had been thrilled when the slim green hardback book marked "author's copy" had come in the mail. At the time he truly believed that the department supported his research, and intended to bring it to clinical use. The reality of rare disease research was that there wasn't enough money to even make producing the compounds or devices worth the time. Larry had continued his work anyway, hoping for some miracle that would allow his findings to actually help patients.

Over the years he became more cynical and even more withdrawn from the important social functions that were critical to an academic scientist's career.

Larry drove his car carefully through the rush hour traffic, glancing around occasionally to see his fellow commuters hunched over the wheel, gripping it tightly as if they could, by sheer will, propel themselves just one further place ahead in the line.

"Lemmings," he thought, "we're all just a bunch of lemmings. What in the world was the point of all of this?" He smiled. "Perhaps I am just having that thing called a midlife crisis."

He recalled the stories of many University researchers who had suddenly lifted their heads from their weary trudging, gone out and bought a motorcycle or a classic car and retired early to tinker in their garages or gardens. Larry thought this kind of story might be an excellent cover for what he was about to do. Rather than just jump ship and go off in search of the Holy Grail of patients who might be able to fund and participate in his research, what if he adopted sort of an alter ego at work until he could tell if this patient advocacy group was really the way to go?

He thought about the games he and his brother used to play in the backyard, dressed in makeshift capes, wielding cardboard shields and garden tools to do battle with the dragons that lurked in the shrubbery.

"Yes, indeed," Larry thought to himself, "I'll take on the role of Midlife Crisis Man. That's a very fine plan!"

He pulled into the driveway and nearly skipped up the walkway to his house. Where to begin? On social media, of course! He booted up the desktop and signed in as a guest user and hesitated for a moment before he realized that it would be better to keep that computer just for research. He pulled out his original phone and typed in the password. Skipping all of the notifications for email and messages, he went instead to the signup page for Twitter.

He chose his screen identity carefully. Using the name

of a kidney disease would allow his tweets to show up in any search a patient or advocacy group might initiate. He typed it in and waited. Available! He composed a brief summary of his decades of work in the disease space and thought about his first tweet. Only 140 characters allowed.

"Thinking of buying a vintage motorcycle with a sidecar to search for patients." Perfect. He pressed the button and leaned back in his chair. This was going to be fun.

He couldn't wait to see the look on the Director's face when the IT folks forwarded these tweets to him. Next, he signed up on Facebook as himself, listing his lab and publications. He joined his high school alumni group and then his college. He considered his first post. What might throw the administrators off of the real purpose of his outreach?

He turned his chair around to face his neatly curated bookshelves. They were organized much like a library catalog system. He pulled his junior high school yearbook off of the shelf and turned the pages slowly. There was a small note in one of the lower right hand corners next to a smiling face.

"Good luck with all of your science, Larry, I hope you save the world!" Sara had been his lab partner in chemistry class. She was very bright and always cheerful, but asked way too many good questions of the teacher and doodled in her notebook.

He clicked on the search box in Facebook and slowly typed in Sara's name. Bingo!

He typed out a friend request. "I think I may be having a midlife crisis, know anybody with a vintage motorcycle with a sidecar for sale? All best, Larry." He clicked on the "send" button.

Now he had established a presence, and he had no idea where it might lead. He powered off the phone and went back to the desktop.

He searched in PubMed for papers more recent than his, or works that had cited his original publication. There weren't many search results, but most of them, oddly enough, were from the University of Helsinki in Finland. He created a folder and saved the references. Although his brain was spinning, he thought he'd better get some sleep to prepare for the fallout at work the next day. He fell asleep easily and slept deeply, for the first time in ages.

The next day he woke up without an alarm and went through his usual morning routine before work, with one major exception. He did not power up his phone. It was hard not to do, but he was determined to just show up at work as if he had completely forgotten to check in.

He pulled into the parking deck and slid into his usual space. He straightened his tie and walked purposefully to his office. No sooner had he turned the key in the lock than he heard the Director running down the hall. He stepped inside the office and shut the door. He sat down at his desk and booted up the computer.

"Three, two, one." he counted silently until the Director burst in to his office.

"Larry" he huffed, nearly foaming at the mouth "why haven't you responded to any of my emails or messages?"

Larry looked up, trying to appear confused. "Oh, sorry," he said carefully, "I was just preoccupied with a research grant idea. I think it will be a big one."

The Director began to salivate. "Really? How big do you think? Enough to make our target?"

Larry leaned back in his chair and put his hands behind his head. "It's too early to tell. I'm just in the preliminary stages of the idea. I really need some time to flesh this out. It's a bold strategy that I'm sure will interest the Head of the Department. I'll need some time to get the proposal together and I'd appreciate it if you'd keep it under wraps for now."

The Director puffed himself up a little. "I'm glad you are taking my SWOT analysis to heart Larry, we really should make a collaborative effort to run this up the flag pole at the next department meeting."

Larry could see the Director had taken the bait. "I may need to go to Bethesda to form a working group with some of the NIH folks. Can you clear the way to fund that trip?"

The Director frowned. "Well, I don't know Larry, I would need to see some justification for that kind of expense..." he trailed off and shifted his weight from one foot to the other.

Larry turned back to his computer. "Think about it, won't you? These translational medicine grants are prestigious, with big bucks for the departments that land them." He began to type in his passwords "Now if you will excuse me, I have work to catch up on."

The Director stepped back out into the hallway and closed the door.

Larry smiled and opened his email box. He clicked on all of the emails from the day before and marked them as read without opening them. Then he went to the grants folder and entered a new document. "Translational medicine funding grants for rare diseases." He started to search the University database for open grant opportunities and copied the largest grants he could find into the document. He spent the morning ignoring emails and filling up the document. He could almost feel the breath on his neck, knowing that each keystroke was being monitored and salivated over by the Director.

At lunchtime he went for a walk around the campus, something he hadn't done in years. He was shocked to see the waves of bicyclists and people running to their next meeting with headphones on, talking into their devices, frantically trying to get there first.

He decided to go to the reference library and see if his thesis was still there. His ID card allowed him access and he couldn't help but notice all of the cameras following him on their swivel mounts as he walked back to the reference desk. "Excuse me" he said quietly to the young woman at the desk "can you direct me to the…"

She pointed to a screen on the counter. "Go ahead and log in here with your ID badge, please, we can proceed from there."

Larry slid his badge through the slot on the side of the screen. The last date of his visit? He couldn't begin to guess. He clicked on the help icon.

The screen blinked once and then said there was no record of him having visited in the past ten years. Would he like to set up a new user account?

Larry didn't think he did, but then he remembered his plan. He went through the process and swiped his ID badge again.

"Access granted!" the screen proclaimed. "What would you like to search for?"

Larry slowly typed in the title of the rare disease publication he had found from Finland.

The cursor on the screen blinked for nearly a minute. "That record is located in off site storage," it said. "Would you like us to retrieve it and notify you when it is available?"

"Oh yes please," said Larry, pushing the accept button, "that would be great."

An innovative international collaborative consortium. That ought to get the Director's attention. Larry did a quick search for his thesis. It was in off site storage as well.

He logged out of the system and turned back to the young woman at the desk. "Is there still a periodical section where I can read newspapers?"

She frowned. "You mean actual historical newspapers? Those are archived and have been digitally scanned. You can access them from your account."

Larry shook his head. "No, I want to read this week's papers from Helsinki, is that possible?"

She frowned again. "I'm not sure" she said carefully, eyeing his badge "let me get someone who might be able to help you."

"Oh that's okay," said Larry a little too brightly, "I'll just search them online from my office, thanks."

She turned away from him and began typing into her workstation.

Larry tried to look dejected for the cameras as he walked back out of the library into the sunshine.

It felt great to walk, and he took the long way to the cafeteria. He got a tray and stood in line and inched his way up to the salad bar.

"The usual, Larry?" said the young man at the counter.

"Nope, I'm thinking of branching out. How about the pickled herring on rye?"

"Wow, that is a stretch. We usually only get that request from Pekka, and he's not due here for another 30 minutes. Let me see if I can make another order. Do you mind stepping out of the line?"

Larry was shocked at how well the plan was working. Who was Pekka and what kind of research was he working on here at the University? This might escalate even faster than he had hoped.

A plate appeared on his tray. "There you go, Larry, enjoy! I'll have to let Pekka know he has competition for the herring now."

"Thanks," said Larry, "a little competition is good for the marketplace, right?" He stepped into the beverage line and filled a glass with unsweetened iced tea and moved with the crowd to the lines for payment. He swiped his card and it beeped uncharacteristically.

The manager looked at him carefully. "Are we going to need to order more herring, or is this just a one time fling?"

Larry thought for just a moment and said, "I'm not sure how long this midlife crisis thing is supposed to last. You might want to order more herring."

The manager laughed and clicked quickly on his key-pad.

Larry hadn't realized how predictable he'd been. He'd never really considered that the salad he ordered was always in stock and that the food prep folks knew what time certain people came in for lunch.

He sat down and ate his sandwich. It was absolutely delicious, and his mind slipped back to the year he had spent in Helsinki during his graduate school work. Yes, this was going to be a fine, fine plan indeed.

Larry spent the rest of the day working diligently in his office, filling out forms, responding to administrative emails and rearranging things on his desk. He was astonished at the amount of time all of this busywork took. If he were to truly keep track of the percentage of time his research was allowed in a regular 40 hour work week, what would that look like?

A reminder popped up on his screen "Departmental meeting 8AM tomorrow."

"Hmmmm." He decided to take this game to the next level. He picked up the phone and punched in the extension number of the Resources Director.

"Hello, Phil? I'm sorry for the late notice, but I won't be able to make the meeting tomorrow morning. I'm not feeling well at all. Would you add an item to the grant proposals in process? International consortium for the sequencing of rare kidney disease patients and the establishment of a genetic database. Yes, thank you. Greatly appreciated." Larry hung up the phone before there were any more questions.

He had already opened a file under that same heading when he came in to the office first thing this morning. He supposed he ought to spend the rest of the day searching for matching grant opportunities just to keep the monitors happy, but that wasn't the way most of the grants were written in this era of reduced funding.

The way he understood it from the meetings, the entire proposal should be written first, with a timeline and milestones, the way the Business School people approached funders, and then someone from the department would lobby the idea around at the high level meetings.

This whole shift had come when they inserted MBA types into every department, supposedly to make things more efficient. It gave Larry a headache in almost every departmental meeting to hear these young, ambitious graduate students cheerleading the benefits of lean manufacturing principles to go along with their PowerPoint presentations.

Tomorrow would be the first departmental meeting he had missed in more than 20 years. He glanced at the clock on his screen. Almost 5pm. His new plan involved a precise 40-hour workweek.

After all, according to these principles of Lean business he'd been hearing about in the meetings, it was essential to have something called a "work life balance." He might even use his sick leave accumulated over all of these years.

He packed up the items on his desk, put them into the locking drawers and stood up slowly. He took off his white lab coat, monogrammed with his name and title. As he was hanging it up on the hook on the back of the office door, a wave of doubt swept over him. What was he thinking? He had worked so hard over the years to be the scientist that his parents would have been proud of....was he throwing it all away? Despite his increasing heart rate and sweaty palms, he locked his office and headed out of the building.

The administrator at the front desk looked up and then at her screen clock. "Larry? Are you alright?"

He felt the sweat begin to drip off of his forehead. "I'm not feeling well at all, Melinda, please cancel anything on my calendar for tomorrow. Thank you." He wiped his brow with the sleeve of his suit coat.

Melinda nodded and said brightly, "I hope it isn't the virus that has been going around. It's a doozy, I hear." She wiped her hands vigorously with the gel-based anti-germ concoction she always kept on her desk and waved to him. "You have plenty of sick time, just call in and let me know if you are going to be out more than three days, okay? Forms to fill out and all of that."

Larry nodded and walked slowly to his car.

He drove carefully toward home and halfway there realized he'd better stop and get something at the grocery store. He bought tea, honey, chicken soup, a dozen organic cage free vegetarian-fed local eggs and some cough and cold lozenges with zinc. They were guaranteed to shorten the duration of a cold or your money back. He tried not to smile.

The cashier glanced at the contents of his shopping cart "Did you find everything okay? Do you have one of our customer rewards cards? You get double points for the zinc lozenges today! It only takes a minute!"

Larry nodded and pulled his reading glasses out of his shirt pocket. He filled out the form, signed and dated it, and handed it back to the cashier. She was wringing her hands with the same gel that Melinda ordered by the case. He noticed it was at every checkout station. He shook his head.

"Everything okay?" chirped the cashier.

"Oh yes, I'm probably just overtired" said Larry as he swiped his new rewards card through the slot.

"Well, if you come in on Wednesdays before 4pm you get double bonus senior discounts as well!" She turned away and began the script with the next customer in line.

Larry thanked the bagger and declined the offer for help out to his car. He lifted the bag of groceries out of the basket and replaced the cart in the corral with all of the others.

A young man in a reflective vest quickly wiped down the handle of the cart with gloved hands and waved cheerfully. "Have a nice day, sir. Drive carefully."

Larry waited until he was inside his car to giggle. It had been a long time since he had been a regular customer in a grocery store. Clearly they had MBAs advising them on their "user experience" as well. The antimicrobial fervor was a little alarming to him. Perhaps that was the reason these viruses kept getting stronger and lasting longer.

He said out loud to the reflection in his rear view mirror "You are off duty, Larry."

As he swung the car into the driveway, his neighbor looked at him over her glasses. "Wow, I don't think I've ever seen you in the daylight on a week day, Larry, you okay?"

He nodded in her direction and gathered the grocery bag from the back seat. "Feeling like I might be coming down with something, a little feverish, but thanks for asking. Everything okay with you?"

She backed away from him. "Don't bring any of those super bugs back from the hospital Larry, you could wipe out the whole neighborhood."

Larry started to smile and dismiss her fears, but she had already run back into her house. He heard the deadbolt click firmly. He sighed and walked into his house.

Once he had closed the door behind him, he allowed himself to grin. This was working spectacularly well. He hadn't had any idea that he would have so many accomplices to his plan. He rubbed his hands together and started the water boiling for tea.

His new phone in his pocket began to buzz. He had three new notifications on his Facebook page! He stood up a little straighter.

He was popular! Somebody remembered him at least. He scrolled through the friend requests. The names sounded vaguely familiar. He'd have to cross-reference them with the yearbook.

The last one nearly made him drop the phone. The patient advocacy group was inviting him to like and follow their page.

The teapot began to whistle urgently. He clicked the "like" and "follow" and "allow updates" buttons and turned off the burner on the stove. His shoulders relaxed. This was going to be a marvelous adventure, he just knew it.

CHAPTER TWO

The next two days were filled with catching up on so many things he hadn't even realized had been ignored. He changed the water filter cartridge in the refrigerator and the batteries in the smoke detectors. Going through his closet, he bagged up all of the clothing he rarely wore or had become threadbare and marked the bags "donate." He read the top two books on the pile that was leaning precariously on the side table next to his bed. He lurked on Facebook and scrolled past all of his former classmates' photos with their grandchildren and their pets and their travel descriptions.

There were a few friend requests each day, and he made small green dots in the yearbook to try and remember who these people were as he accepted their requests.

He posted on Twitter that he was feeling under the weather and searched for the lab page in Finland where he had done his postdoc work. Amazingly, there were updates.

The Finns spoke better English than most of his American colleagues, and as he remembered, had a particular lack of competition with each other. There was more of a sense of drive for the good of the country and their fellow citizens. He had thoroughly enjoyed the open discussions and the sharing of results in those days, and hadn't really appreciated how different it would be from the rest of his career as a scientist.

The work of a lifetime was something the Finns just got up everyday and did, without any sense of entitlement or lack thereof. There was very little waste, of time or energy or resources. The environment was harsh but strangely beautiful to him at the time, and he felt a sudden longing for the deep dark nights of the Finnish winter.

The temperature-controlled environment of his current life meant you could go for years without ever really knowing what day or time it was. The lights and lack of open spaces meant that the stars were hardly ever visible.

Finns seemed to know where they were in space at any given moment. They shaded their eyes with their hands and looked to the skies. They knew what the wind direction was and what that meant in terms of weather. The Northern Lights had been one of the highlights of Larry's life. He could still see the greenish blue gradient if he closed his eyes. He knew he was romanticizing the country, and holding them up on a pedestal as a culture was probably a gross generalization, but he wondered what it was like in their Universities these days. Perhaps this international collaborative consortium grant would take him to Finland again and he would be able to see for himself.

After three days of chicken soup and tea, and a much cleaner house, Larry went back to work. He slid back into the routine as if nothing or nobody had missed him. He spent his mornings reading papers and creating a reference list for his grant. He went to endless meetings and made cryptic notes in his notebook. He nodded at colleagues and lowered his head as he walked quickly with all of the other earnest seekers of knowledge streaming in predictable traffic patterns around the campus. He went back to his regular time and order at the cafeteria.

He asked Melinda what paperwork he needed to fill out to attend a workshop for continuing education in Bethesda.

She handed him a folder and smiled brightly. "Things going well, Larry? I hear you have a big grant proposal."

Larry nodded, hoping to appear distracted and deep in thought. "It's coming along," he said, drifting back toward his office.

Melinda frowned. She took great pride in knowing the very latest gossip, and felt as if the entire department depended on her to hold it together. She would tell you so if you gave her even the slightest opening in any conversation. How she had been with the department for twenty long years, underpaid and under appreciated. "I mean really, what would these man babies do if I weren't keeping them in line?" she'd whine.

Larry tried to be pleasant with her and acknowledge her steadfast loyalty to the endless grind of paperwork that kept the money flowing to the department. He bristled when she tried to learn more about his family or his personal life, but it didn't take much to get her right back on her bandwagon of "what would happen to this place without me" monologues.

He had seen several arrogant colleagues run afoul of her and the consequences had not been pretty. Whatever her relationship was with the department chairman was a mystery to Larry, but everybody whispered about the possibilities.

Was there something she knew that would be blackmail material?

He shook his head quickly, not letting that train of thought continue. In many ways, the department was just like his memories of middle school chemistry class. The clamoring for attention from the teacher, the kids who sat in the back and openly copied from each other's notes, the clowns who set things on fire for attention. Nothing had changed much.

He remembered how enthused he had been about a life in science after reading biographies about Edison and Einstein from the public library. It had seemed like the discoveries were surrounded by a life of literate and fascinating conversation, and great camaraderie.

The reality had been a shock in the first few years. The endless unproductive meetings, the squabbles over resources, the paperwork. Oh God, the paperwork.

Larry sighed deeply and went back into his office with the folder of required paperwork necessary to get him to Bethesda and the National Institutes of Health. He felt like there was a small window of time when he might still be able to get his work taken seriously and he needed to go through the motions to make that happen. He knew the possibility was small indeed, but he thought about the patients and their advocacy group. What would it mean to them if he could pull this off? He opened the folder and began to fill out the forms. At 5pm, he stopped, closed the folder and put it in the locking top drawer of his desk. He locked his office, walked quickly past Melinda with his phone to his ear as if he were listening to an important message, and bolted out of the building.

Larry kept this schedule up for weeks, 40 hours per week at the office. Melinda stopped looking at him strangely and stopped asking questions when he submitted the paperwork.

Her eyes widened when she saw the folder the first time. "Wow, Larry, that's a pretty ambitious proposal," she said rather loudly "I really hope it works out. It would mean a lot to the department."

Larry nodded and kept walking. He wondered who was listening to those conversations and whether all of the security cameras had audio capabilities. Regardless, he knew there were much bigger issues within the department keeping the security folks busy, so hopefully he was just going along with the flow, under the radar so to speak.

In the evenings he worked feverishly on the proposal

for the patient advocacy group. He filled folders on the desktop computer with obscure papers from around the world that had cited his research or were relevant to his interests. He made lists of possible collaborators and read their publications.

Larry was struck by how often there was no mention of any negative results. So many grants, so many experiments, just never continued. He knew why. For the same reason his had not continued when he went down that same road in his early research. Why wasn't anybody talking about not reinventing the wheel? He tried to imagine bringing something like that up in a departmental meeting. It would be career suicide.

He allowed himself to dream about an open access policy that would actually publish all of the results, positive and negative, and move toward reproducibility of results. Would that be more likely in the Finnish system? Could he even broach the subject? He started another folder, "Open Access Journals" and began to search for people who were working on the idea. It would take a huge funding operation to step outside of the profitable "publish or perish" model and he wasn't sure what the selling point would be. Obviously, if there was a large enough patient population with a celebrity who could leverage the public interest.... Larry remembered the Jerry Lewis telethons and the juvenile diabetes fundraisers. How had they gotten off the ground?

It seemed like a long shot, but he hoped there might be a Finnish sports superstar who might be interested in championing the cause if there was someone in his family with the disease. How unlikely that would be, but Larry allowed himself to brainstorm along those lines. He opened up another folder, named it "Finnish collaborators" and realized he had been limiting himself to scientists in his field. What if he opened up the parameters to include people with personal experience, or approached it from other avenues than academic medicine?

He felt a sudden lightness of being, as if he had risen above the system, just for a moment. Perhaps it was time to get some sleep.

He tossed and turned that night, dreaming of roaming the countryside, looking for an honest man. In his dream he was holding a lamp and trudging through the snow. Surely this was an epic poem he had read in his undergraduate days, or a movie he had seen, he thought in the shower the next morning. He had never cast himself as the hero in his own epic drama before. Perhaps that was the impetus for most midlife crisis behavior after all.

As Larry drove to the office, he thought about what it might mean to work outside the system. He'd have to learn to grocery shop, of course, and prepare his own meals. It seemed ludicrous to even be thinking about independence, considering how dependent he was on the University.

He pulled into the parking garage and began to walk briskly towards the campus. Perhaps a good walk would clear his head. He flashed his badge at the sensors on his office building and walked awkwardly into the glass double doors. He tried again. The doors were locked. He glanced at the keypad.

"Report to Administrative Office" it flashed in bright red alphanumeric characters.

Larry groaned. The last time he had needed to replace his badge it had taken the better part of two days. He started off toward the administrative offices and hardly noticed when a large man joined him and took his arm by the crook of the elbow. Larry flinched, and then saw it was his friend Albert. "Hey Al, what's up with you?" Larry said lightly "Awfully early for you to be on campus, isn't it?"

Albert was as pale as Larry had ever seen him. "No laughing matter Larry, let's get to the big guy's office as quickly as possible, okay?"

Larry was confused. What in the world was going on? Perhaps there had been some security breach.

Albert worked for the legal department and handled "all manner of irregularities" as he referred to them.

"What is going on, Albert?"

"Can't tell you until we are inside, Larry. It's pretty serious, though."

They went quickly up the stairs to the third floor, where the head of the department had a corner office with sweeping views of the campus. Larry and Albert were ushered inside, where they were joined by two other high-ranking administrators.

The head of the department was behind his desk, his head in his hands. He looked up slowly. "Thanks for coming, Larry. I'll just assume you haven't heard anything and lay out the facts for you. Sit down, please."

The chair he motioned to was directly across from him, and Larry thought for a moment he might be about to get fired. Had he missed the 40-hour per week mark somehow? He felt a little ill.

"Larry, I am not sure how to begin, so I will just start with yesterday's events. At about 8:30 last night, one of our colleagues in the department, Dr. Rodriguez, was found unconscious in his office by one of the cleaning staff. He was later pronounced dead at the hospital."

Larry started to jump up out of his chair. "Oh my goodness!"

"Sit down Larry, it gets much worse." The head of the department ran his fingers through what was left of his hair. "We've been concerned about some issues over the last few weeks, and apparently, well, there is no other way to say this, Dr. Rodriguez was poisoned. The police have taken Melinda into custody and there is an ongoing investigation."

Larry looked around the room. Albert and the other administrators nodded and hung their heads. Larry could not find the words to speak.

The department head held up his hand. "We're all in shock, Larry. Melinda has been a loyal and dedicated part of this department for many years. We had no reason to suspect that there was anything amiss. Dr. Rodriguez brought some things to my attention about a month ago, and I was reluctant to believe him. He is a young, ambitious, oh excuse me, was a scientist with a very bright future. We have only begun to uncover some of what has been going on here in the department, and unfortunately the irregularities extend beyond the affair with Dr. Rodriguez and Melinda. Larry, I have no idea how she was able to manipulate the system, but Melinda has, over the years, cost this department dearly in what we thought were rejected grant applications. Rather than do the paperwork necessary to submit the grants, she was somehow able to get ahold of the rejection letter templates from the granting agencies, and simply sent them to some of our colleagues instead of completing her work. She was very careful, and I am disappointed to have to tell you that you have been the recipient of some of those fraudulent rejection notices."

Larry slumped in the chair.

The department head continued. "Larry, I cannot imagine how this must feel. You have done excellent work, and your research should have been continuously funded. I have no earthly idea why Melinda would have targeted you and your research, but we are prepared today to offer you some kind of," he glanced at Albert who mouthed the word "compensation" "yes, compensation for your losses. I'll let Albert take over from here. I'm still reeling from all of this, you understand Larry. I haven't slept a wink, and,"

Albert interrupted him. "Under the terms of your employment with the University, there are certain clauses which prohibit you from disclosing information that might be harmful to the Institution. There are further clauses that provide you with full legal protection in the event of any wrongdoing by clerical or administrative staff. We are prepared to offer you a very generous severance package, with full retirement at the end of the year, and a leave of absence until then, if you will agree to not sue the Institution and not disclose these terms. We are also prepared to waive your noncompeting terms so that you are free to seek employment of your choosing. We will give you the highest recommendations and stand behind your work. You will need to sign a few documents, which we have prepared for you." Albert could not look him in the eye.

Larry started to stand up. "I'll need a few days to think this over," he began.

Albert walked over and put his hand on his shoulder, forcing him to sit down again. "No, Larry, that is not an option. You will sign these papers now, and be excused from testifying at a trial that could potentially devastate your career and the careers of others in the department. We really have no other option."

Larry sighed, and slid forward in his chair, pulling his reading glasses out of his shirt pocket. "I will at least, be allowed to read the documents before I sign them, though, is that correct?"

Albert nodded. "Of course Larry. We are not doing anything but trying to protect you and your research. These are merely formalities to allow you to continue your work."

Larry looked at Albert. This time his gaze was returned. Larry flinched. Albert looked as if he had been crying for many hours.

Larry began to read the documents. He was being given an extraordinary chance. He knew that somehow his dream was being realized thanks to these awful circumstances, but he was determined to remain as calm as possible and go along with whatever adventure this wild ride took him on. After a few pages, he asked Albert to explain one of the clauses. It appeared that the University had much more to lose if Larry sued them. He was in the driver's seat. "I'd like to ask for one more thing" he said, his voice wavering. "I've been working on a consortium idea that requires me to go to Bethesda to meet with some other scientists in the field. The conference is at the end of February. I've already prepared the paperwork."

"Yes, Larry, we found them in your desk." the department head sighed. "If you'll keep reading, you'll see that we've granted that request out of the funds of the department. You will not have to submit any further paperwork for that conference."

Larry moved all the way to the front of the chair and read the entire document. He could scarcely believe what he was being offered. He turned to Albert again. "I know you cannot advise me, Albert, but is there anything else I am prohibited from doing?"

Albert shook his head slowly. "No, Larry, we are just glad that you are not among Melinda's victims beyond the sabotage of your research. We really are trying to compensate you for your loss." He looked directly at Larry "We are also aware that you and your research may be very attractive to a pharma company or other for-profit groups. You are free to explore those options as well."

Larry nodded "Thank you Albert. This is all too much to process, but I understand that this is a good faith offer. I will sign the paperwork. Will I need to turn in my keys and my badge?"

Albert shook his head again "No Larry, you will have full rights and privileges as a researcher here at the University until the end of the year. We will announce your retirement at that time. It is our deepest hope that you will have other employment well before then." He handed Larry a pen. The document was signed and witnessed by all present in the room.

Larry stood up and extended his hand to the department chairman across the desk. "Thank you Clif, it really has been an honor and a privilege to work with you. I truly appreciate all of your support for my work. I had begun to feel like I was not really,"

Clif interrupted him "I know, Larry. I am deeply sorry. You cannot imagine what this feels like to me. My whole career and the careers of my department colleagues meant the world to me." He sat down and began to sob.

Albert took Larry's elbow again and guided him out of the room. In the hallway, directly under the security camera he said a little too loudly "You are under no obligation to answer any questions Larry. This is an active investigation and all questions should be directed to me." He handed Larry his business card. "Thank you for coming in and answering our questions, Larry. Why don't you take the rest of the week off? The building will be an active investigation site, and no work is going to get done anyway. Feel free to reach out to me if you need anything." He shook Larry's hand firmly.

They turned away from each other. Larry walked slowly to the parking structure. He could not believe what he had just heard. Surely his alarm would go off any minute now and he would wake up and take a shower and start his day. He glanced at his watch. It was nearly noon.

Larry reached his car on shaky legs, and as he sat in the driver's seat, he began to shake uncontrollably. He managed to pull the door shut, and leaned his head back against the headrest. He tried to slow his breathing, calm himself down. He shook his head to clear it, and put the key in the ignition.

Although he wasn't entirely sure it was safe to do so, he backed out of the space and headed for home. His mind was racing. He turned on the radio to the classical music station. He felt his shoulders relax a little bit as the soothing music washed over him. He tried to relax his grip on the steering wheel, and focus on the road ahead. He saw the shopping center entrance up ahead and pulled in to the parking lot.

Just before he turned off the ignition, the noon news came on the radio. He sat and listened as the announcer began "In a bizarre murder-suicide, two University employees have died. Police confirm that there have been multiple calls to domestic violence incidents in the past few weeks involving the two, but no arrest had been made. Preliminary toxicology reports indicate that a researcher was poisoned, and an administrator died in police custody of the same poison. Names are being withheld pending family notification. A spokesperson for the University declined to comment, citing an active investigation. There appears to be no threat to the University system or the public's safety. In weather news,"

Larry switched off the ignition.

He struggled to slow his breathing. Perhaps a brisk walk would help him calm down. He got out of the car and walked around the complex, forcing himself to look in the windows of the shops, trying not to bump into any of the shoppers out on their lunch breaks. He counted his inhales and exhales, trying to keep them even. Nobody seemed to be aware that anything untoward had happened just down the road. Larry wasn't even sure he was aware of what exactly had happened. After a few laps around the complex, Larry stopped in a small bookshop. He browsed the best sellers and periodicals before heading back to the science section. His vision blurred as he tried to scan the titles, looking for what he wasn't sure of, a sign maybe, that things would return to normal.

A clerk nodded to him as he headed back out of the bookstore empty handed.

He made it to his car and took a few deep breaths. Perhaps the grocery store would make the most sense. Could he navigate it? Only one way to find out.

He gripped the wheel and forced himself to concentrate on the trip. He kept the radio off now, not wanting to hear any more news. He tried to replay the conversation from Clif's office in his head and square it with the news that he had just heard. He couldn't help but replay the statement about how lucky he was not to have been among Melinda's victims beyond the sabotage of his research.

Victims? Who else had suffered in this weird series of events? How long had it been going on? What was going on?

Larry realized he was rocking back and forth, almost touching the steering wheel with his torso. He tried to relax his arms. He tried to slow his breathing. The short trip to the grocery store seemed an eternity at this point. He needed to calm down.

Finally, the grocery store parking lot came into view. He pulled into a parking space some distance from the entrance and walked unsteadily to the cart corral. He pulled out a cart and leaned on it for stability. He walked up and down the aisles, trying to figure out what he would need in this new life he was about to embark upon.

He bought the staples. Eggs, bread, cheese, salad in a bag, olive oil, vinegar, a rotisserie chicken. Apples, some pears, and a few carrots from the produce section. That was all he could manage for today. He pushed the cart to the checkout line and leaned on it heavily as he waited his

turn. He tried to imagine what he would say to his neighbors. They probably had heard the news by now and
would be full of questions. He remembered what Albert
had said and realized he would need to practice saying
those words. "It's an active investigation, I can't really
comment."

His turn came to pay for his groceries.

"Do you have your rewards card?" the cashier chirped
"Just slide it through there, or I can look it up by your
phone number."

Larry slid the card through the side of the keypad and
waited for the beep. His groceries moved past him on a
conveyor belt, and were bagged up. He paid his bill, declined the offer for help out to his car, and walked purposefully with his bags to the car. It had seemed like that
took hours to complete, but he had done it.

The first step in his new life as a retired researcher.
Larry slumped at the thought. This could, and should be
his big opportunity, to finally work with patients and perhaps even a pharma company with the resources to bring
his work to the clinic. Why did these awful things have to
happen to open the door for this opportunity?

Larry began to feel angry. Angry at all the time he had
wasted under the delusion that the University would support him and his research and eventually fund the translation to patients.

Had it all been a big lie? Was it just all about funding
the layers of administration and people like Melinda, who
ultimately had far more control over his research than he
did? How could this have happened? Larry's head began
to pound. At least she hadn't poisoned him. There was
that to be thankful for, he guessed. Essentially though, she
had poisoned his career, and who knows how many others?

Larry tried to think about all of the promising researchers who had been heavily recruited who hadn't stayed in the department very long before taking jobs in other places. He had been so focused on his own grant writing and paper submissions that he hadn't really paid much attention, but now that he began to think about it, the list was long.

The monthly department meetings were often started with announcements of new researchers. Very rarely was anything mentioned about the departing colleagues. There were whispered rumors about some of the departures, but Larry had tried to keep his distance from the office politics. Perhaps he should have paid more attention. Or perhaps, ignorance really was bliss, and he had managed to survive by focusing on his own work. He relaxed a little, and pulled into his driveway. No neighbors in sight.

He grabbed the bags of groceries and walked quickly into the house, locking the door behind him. He put away the groceries and began to clean the house.

He was expecting the police or the reporters, or even the neighbors, at any moment to knock on the door and start asking him questions about what had happened at work. About what he knew, or didn't know. At least the house might be presentable by the time they arrived. Larry wiped down the counters, vacuumed and dusted.

He looked around and realized it was like a small time capsule in his house. The furniture from his parents' house, arranged in just the way it had been in the living room when he was in high school. He ran his hand along the back of the couch. It had been comforting to set all of this up after his parents had died, but all of these years later, was he still just living like a college student? At least he hadn't stocked up on ramen noodles at the grocery store. He tried to laugh at his own joke. It wasn't very funny though, was it? Two people had just died, and he had been essentially let go by the department. It wasn't funny at all.

He went through the motions of making himself dinner, although he wasn't the least bit hungry. He plugged his phones into their charging stations and booted up the desktop computer. He tried to work on the patient advocacy group's proposal, but his eyes kept blurring, and his heart just wasn't in it. He managed to open a new folder titled "Rare Disease Day, Bethesda Maryland." At least he had that to look forward to. In the meantime, he was feeling absolutely exhausted. He shut down the computer, turned off the lights, and headed for his bedroom. The clock by his bed said it was only 7pm. Larry decided perhaps he would just lie down for a little while, give his mind a chance to rest. He fell into a deep sleep almost immediately.

The next morning he felt as though he had a wicked case of jet lag. He couldn't focus on what day or time it was. He checked his phones for messages. Nothing. His email was mostly junk, the usual offers for subscriptions to questionable scientific journals and meetings to attend. His calendar had been updated with a notification. He clicked on it.

The regular reminder for the departmental meeting had been cancelled. "Do you wish to accept this cancellation or reply to sender?"

He clicked "accept" and sighed deeply. Under any other circumstances, the freedom of not having to go to any more departmental meetings would have been cause for celebration. He felt deeply guilty for his plans to have feigned a midlife crisis. He certainly hadn't expected any of this real life drama.

He went into the kitchen to make coffee. He guessed he should feel lucky to be alive, but at the moment he just felt like a bus had hit him. He paced back and forth across the kitchen tiles, being careful not to step on the grout lines while waiting for the beep that signaled the coffee was ready. He poured a cup and drank it quickly, as if it was any other morning and he would be heading out the door shortly to go to the office. Only this wasn't any other morning, and Larry had no idea how he was going to function without his long established routine.

Wasn't that what having a midlife crisis was all about? Waking up one morning and deciding to just NOT do the mind numbing routine in service to some corporate goal? Riding off into the sunset on a motorcycle or a horse or a classic car and just saying, "Screw it"? Sending a letter of resignation from some island in the Caribbean? That was how it happened in the movies.

Perhaps he had known deep down that something was going to happen and.... no, that was ridiculous. He couldn't have known or imagined anything like this.

Now he poured himself another cup of coffee and gave himself a good stern talking to. "Larry, you have a chance to realize your dream of working with patients toward a cure. The circumstances may not be what you had hoped for, or wished on anybody, but don't waste the opportunity when it knocks on your door."

He nodded. He straightened his shoulders, marched himself off to get a shower and get dressed and start the day as if it were any other day, except he would be working from home.

He'd put in the hours he had been committed to, 40 hours per week, and start making plans to meet with the patient advocacy group. Maybe not today, but he would set a goal for the next, what seemed appropriate, two weeks? He showered and shaved and put on his usual suit and tie, and walked to his study instead of driving to work.

It felt weird at first, but over the next two weeks, when there wasn't any more news in the paper or on the television, and nobody came to the door to ask any questions, Larry settled into his research and a routine that seemed reasonable.

He still felt waves of grief and anger over what might have been had his career not been sabotaged, but he bolstered himself with the assertion that he was still alive, and able to make a difference if he kept at it. One foot in front of the other, one day at a time. That's how he had gotten through the rigors of graduate school and his PhD studies, and the deaths of his parents, and he'd just have to keep trudging along like a good soldier through this, too.

At the end of the first week, he allowed himself to check in on the department website from his phone. He was curious if he really did still had full privileges as he had been promised, and if there was any news, or statement from the chair.

He was shocked to find that the website had been completely revamped. All traces of Melinda and Dr. Rodriguez were gone. In Melinda's place was a young man named David, a first year graduate of the school of business with a concentration in social media marketing. Larry groaned. He allowed himself to scroll through the page where the researchers were listed. Next to his name it said "currently on sabbatical" and provided a link to his publications.

Larry quickly closed the browser and put the phone back on its charger. His heart was racing and he felt a little queasy. What did one do on a sabbatical? Was he expected to do some brilliant piece of work and let the University PR folks spin it as another breakthrough?

He stood up and paced around the house for a few minutes to try and calm himself down. He knew what he had to do. He had to make plans to go to the Rare Disease Day conference and meet the patients and their advocates to try and get his work funded through a partnership. That was his work from this point forward.

He sat back down at his desk with a fresh cup of coffee and began to draft an outline. He refused to use any of the "let's take a 30,000 ft. view of the current roadmap" kind of jargon that had infiltrated most of the recent conferences he had attended. They were usually poorly disguised junkets in lovely places where spouses and children could attend and feel somehow appeased that their family member had to work such long hours for such low pay. He wouldn't even use PowerPoint slides.

"How rebellious," he thought, dryly. "I'm really getting into this midlife crisis thing; maybe I'll even stop shaving for a week."

He doubted he would actually do that, but it helped his mood a little bit as he worked through the goals and objectives, set some milestones and a reasonable timeline. He was stumped when he came to the funding portion of it. He left his salary blank, and hoped he could come back to that part later.

There had been a recent scandal when a researcher had asked for first class plane tickets and a $30,000 stipend for a lecture to industry leaders looking to invest in a particular therapeutic development scheme. The outpouring of disbelief and vitriol from scientists on social media had been mildly amusing to Larry.

He couldn't even get his reimbursement for carfare to the continuing education meeting approved. He hadn't stayed overnight in the conference hotel because it had been too expensive even if it had been reimbursed. He guessed he was becoming one of those old guys who told the stories about gas being 35 cents a gallon and walking uphill both ways to school in the snow.

He stood up to do some more pacing. Where would his career be now if his grants had been funded and his lab was still operational? Would pharma groups have courted him with offers to join them? Would he have accepted those offers? He'd never know, obviously, but he felt himself grinding his teeth, a habit he'd had in his early career days, causing horrible headaches. The employee health service had fitted him with a mouth guard and recommended that he do some cognitive behavioral therapy, which had helped immensely. Perhaps it was time to go back and see the therapist again. The circumstances certainly warranted it. Larry made a note on his long-term to do list. He relaxed his jaw and got back to the outline.

The next task was to describe the ideal lab setup he would need to efficiently do the work necessary to bring results to a clinical setting. He had no idea where to begin. It had been so long since he had been in an efficient lab designed to produce results other than those for publication and University "Atta boy" points.

He felt his jaw begin to clench again. He stood up and paced a few laps around the kitchen island. Perhaps it was time for a lunch break. He made some chicken salad, spread it on stale rye crackers and washed it down with a couple of large glasses of water. He took some Aleve as well, hoping to stave off the headache he could feel beginning behind his temples.

He went into the bedroom and stripped the bed, threw the sheets and pillowcases into a basket and carried them out to the garage to launder them. On the way back to the bedroom, he stopped at the hall closet and found the flannel sheets he usually switched to in the winter, although here in January it was still a pleasant enough temperature. It rarely got down into the 30's.

Larry remembered his teenage years when he dreamed of living in such a climate. One of his goals in graduate school had been to finally get out of the snow and work somewhere that did not require a shovel or a snow blower.

He stopped halfway through putting the fitted sheet on

the bed and stood up straight. He realized he had achieved many of the things that had seemed so out of reach to him when he was filling out those college applications. He needed to start being proud of those things. He finished folding the top sheet back, the way his mother always had, fluffed the pillows and shook the quilt before placing it carefully on top.

His grandmother had made the quilt for him when he went away to college. He had covered it with a sleeping bag in his days in the dorm, but he was extraordinarily proud of it now, so glad it had survived. He stretched and attempted to relax his jaw again.

He spent the afternoon looking at pictures and reading descriptions of the labs at Harvard and MIT. Those places were cold and snowy and crazy competitive, and he wasn't the least bit jealous of the facilities, knowing the price that came along with them.

He might have to pay that price to move to the next level in his career. It didn't hurt to see what the latest state of the art lab looked like though. That was just part of good due diligence, right? He felt like he was looking in the windows of the rich kids' houses and coveting their toys. He needed to get himself off of this pity party wagon and just do the research.

By the time it got dark, he had a pretty good descriptive section for the Lab and Equipment portion of his proposal. He had put in his eight hours. It was time to have some dinner and maybe read a book.

He had just settled in for a good science fiction read, his brother had given him the latest novel by Neal Stephenson for the holidays, when his new notifications ringtone began to chime. He put down the book and went to go turn it off for the evening.

"Sara has added you as a friend" the notification said. Larry's hand shook a little bit as he swiped the notice across the screen to see the direct message that she had sent.

"Hi Larry, sorry for the long delay in my response. I don't know anything about motorcycles, but of course I still want to be friends with you! Hope you are doing well. Please call me when you have a chance. It would be great to hear your voice!"

There was a number with an area code that Larry didn't recognize. He wrote the number down on a post it note and looked at the clock. He'd call her tomorrow.

He went back to his reading chair and picked up the book. He was too distracted to even start reading again. He wondered what Sara was up to these days, what they would talk about. It had been more than 40 years since their chemistry class together. He resisted the urge to turn on the computer and begin searching for information. He didn't want to spoil it. He wanted to hear the story from her.

After trying to remember any pertinent details from all those years ago, Larry shook his head and opened the book again. Better to get lost in a good story tonight. He'd make the connection tomorrow. It didn't take long for Larry to get caught up in the plot, and he allowed himself four delicious chapters before he closed the book and headed for bed.

He'd almost forgotten what it was like to read for pleasure. He'd been a voracious reader while he was growing up, sneaking a flashlight and the latest library books into his room at night, and reading until he could no longer keep his eyes open.

Now that a big part of his job was reading for research, and there was an absolute flood of information being published by the hour, Larry had lost his joy and wonder at the magical worlds of science fiction. Maybe he could get that back again. Get off the treadmill of required reading, so much of it dry and formulaic and full of the buzzwords Larry had come to dread, and go for an adventure to be transported to another galaxy. One that was far, far away. Larry smiled and turned off the light.

He woke up the next morning in a surprisingly good mood. He hummed in the shower. He made himself an omelet with smoked salmon from a tin in the back of the cupboard. He didn't even check the expiration date.

He went to the computer and looked up the area code of Sara's phone number. It was in Virginia. He was glad he hadn't called the night before. It would have been awfully late, and he didn't want to get off on the wrong foot. He waited until he thought it might be lunchtime where she was and dialed the number. He was surprised at how nervous he was. He cleared his throat.

"Hello?" a very pleasant, almost familiar voice answered the phone.

"Hello, Sara, this is Larry. I hope this is a good time for you to talk."

"Oh my goodness, Larry! I didn't think you'd call after I took so long to get back to you. Thank you so much for calling. How are you these days?"

Larry took a deep breath. "I'm well, Sara. I hope you are. I am on sabbatical at the moment and am looking forward to traveling to Bethesda Maryland next month for the Rare Disease Day conference at the NIH. What are you up to?"

"Well," there was a long pause "I'm just now starting to get back to my regular life. I've been a bit of a hermit the last five years or so. This is the first friend thing I've done on Facebook in a very long time. I'm glad it is you, Larry. Please forgive me if I," she said "Tell me about you."

Larry couldn't imagine Sara as a hermit. She had always had an easy way with everybody, cheerful and friendly. "There isn't a lot to tell, Sara, I've been working away on my research for 30 years now, and I'm finally going to get to meet some patients at the Rare Disease Day, so I guess you could say I've been kind of a hermit as well."

"Oh, that sounds really interesting, Larry, tell me about the research."

Larry could hardly believe it. "Really, you want to hear about it? It is kind of boring, most people aren't exactly...."

"No Larry, I'd love to hear about it, really!"

Sara sounded genuinely interested, so Larry began to describe his work with the filters in the kidneys and how difficult it had been to develop a small enough screen from the material he had invented. He went through his timeline of discovery, and the materials lab that he had built and the long hours under the hood at the bench. He stopped suddenly "Sara, are you still there?"

"Oh yes, Larry, it is fascinating. I feel like I have a glimpse into what your world looks like. You describe it so clearly! It must be exciting to be making a difference for patients."

"Well, I hope I am about to be able to make a difference for patients. It has all been theoretical up to this point. I mean I have prototypes of the portable device and proofs of concept, and all of that, but it is not proven yet, not in patients anyway, but I am very hopeful."

Sara sighed "Oh Larry, I am really excited for you. This is the best news I've had in years, really. Thank you so much for sharing it with me. I have to get back to work now, but I'd love to talk to you again. Is this a good time for your schedule?"

"I'm on sabbatical, Sara, my time is my own."

Sara laughed. "Okay, can you call me again at this time on Monday? Unless you think that is too soon? I'm not very good at the reconnection stuff. I feel like I am back in middle school again. In a good way, Larry."

Larry stood up a little straighter "Yes, Sara, I feel like that too. I'd be happy to call you on Monday. Talk to you then, bye for now."

"Bye for now, Larry. That's a lovely way to sign off." Sara hung up the phone.

Larry stood very still for a few moments and then raised his hands in the air. "Yes!" he exclaimed, "She was actually interested in my research and wants me to call her back!"

He felt more hopeful than he had in years. Maybe things really were going to turn around for him. He opened his proposal folders with a renewed purpose.

"Yes," he thought, "I really am about to make the leap from theoretical to practical. It would be exciting to have somebody to share that with."

Larry called Sara every day for the next week on her lunch break. It was such a pleasant way to spend an hour, and Larry began to look forward to it with increasing excitement.

He learned that Sara worked in the Foundation office at the philharmonic symphony orchestra in town, and they reminisced about her adventures with the flute in the school orchestra back in the day.

Larry was delighted to tell her that he had season tickets for the symphony for many years and that he always enjoyed the flute parts. "I guess I've always been thinking of you, Sara. I hope that is okay."

She hesitated. "It's delightful Larry. Truly delightful."

Larry took a deep breath. "Could I call you tomorrow, Sara, and talk a little longer? I don't want to intrude on your weekend, but I really am enjoying these calls."

"Oh Larry, that would be great. Around the same time? I know it is early for you, out there on the left coast and all."

Larry grinned. "I'm always up early, Sara, I'll look forward to our conversation tomorrow. Bye for now!"

Larry felt like his life had a renewed purpose. He was starting to believe that it might actually be possible to tell Sara one of these days that his work had saved a patient's life. Wouldn't that be something? He hardly knew what to think about this recent run of good fortune. Maybe hard work really did pay off after all.

CHAPTER THREE

The next day, Larry was up early, as usual, and listening to classical music on the streaming service through his computer. It was so great that Sara didn't think him stodgy or old-fashioned, she worked for a symphony orchestra, for heaven's sake. He hummed along to the music, directing with an imaginary baton.

He cleaned the house and took out the trash and put a load of laundry in the machine in the garage. He checked his watch. Again. It was still several hours until it was time to call Sara.

He opened up his research folders and began to read the latest Journal of the American Society of Nephrology papers. He glanced at his watch again. Perhaps he should set a timer on his phone. He didn't want to be late. "For a very important date!" he hummed to himself. Finally it was time to call Sara.

He waited until a minute after the hour, and pushed the button next to her contact information to dial the number.

She answered on the second ring. "Hi Larry! What's new in the world of kidneys?"

Larry hesitated for a moment, confused. "Wow, Sara, I was just reading the latest Journal of the American Society of Nephrology articles. How did you know?"

"Oh, I didn't really, Larry. I was just trying to keep the conversation light. This is a really difficult day for me, and I am really glad to have you to talk to."

"Oh, I am sorry, Sara. What makes it difficult?" He heard Sara take a quick breath.

"I guess I should have told you earlier, Larry. It has been so delightful to get to know you again, and I didn't want to take up the time we've had together on my lunch breaks, but I feel like I have to tell you now."

Larry's heart sank. He hoped it wasn't the last phone call they'd have together.

"Larry, five years ago today, my husband and son were killed in a terrible automobile accident. The young woman driving the other car had a seizure disorder of some kind, and crossed the median while having an episode. They were all killed, Larry. I just felt like my world stopped turning that day. He was my only child, they were on their way home from an indoor Special Olympics soccer game."

Larry waited for her to pause. "I'm so sorry Sara. I've never been married and obviously I don't have children. I cannot imagine the pain. I am so sorry."

"Oh, Larry, I appreciate that more than you know. Everybody tells me they understand my pain, and I'll get over it and I need to move on. It is awful. You are the first person who has….who has just listened and been truly sorry. Oh that's not what I mean. Of course people have been sorry. But they act like I have some kind of, I don't know, something contagious that might inflict the tragedy on their family or their child or, gosh, Larry, this is the first time I've talked about this since the accident without sobbing hysterically. Thank you."

Larry tried to think of the right thing to say. "Thank you for trusting me enough to tell me, Sara. I know it must be difficult to feel like people don't understand your pain. I won't pretend I do. It may sound selfish, but I really want to keep talking to you. In fact, I'd like to see you when I am in Maryland at the end of next month. Would you consider it?"

Sara's voice was very quiet and he wasn't sure if she

was crying now. "Yes, Larry. I will consider it. Thank you."

As much as Larry wanted to keep her on the phone for the rest of the day, he realized it would be better for her to have some time to consider this conversation. "Same time tomorrow Sara? Let's just make it a standing date, shall we?"

"Oh yes please, Larry. I'd like that. Bye for now."

Their next few conversations were intentionally light. They talked about the weather, the symphonies they both enjoyed, what they were reading. It turned out that Sara liked science fiction, too. She was particularly interested in Tolkien though, and Larry was stunned when she told him that her mother had been Finnish.

"She met my father at University when he studied in Helsinki for a year. They corresponded and eventually got married and she came over here. I've been to Finland a couple of times when I was younger to visit my grandparents, and when I learned that the Elven languages in the Tolkien books were based on Finnish, I felt like I was part of the story."

Larry told her about his time in Finland, and how he hoped to collaborate with some of the scientists at the University of Helsinki. "It's just amazing to me Sara, just amazing. It feels like I've been waiting for you somehow." Larry felt himself blush.

Sara giggled. "That's so sweet, Larry. I have to say it feels the same to me. Very comforting, like you know me already, and yet, there is still so much to discover. It gives me hope, Larry. Thank you."

Larry looked forward to their phone calls, and realized how lucky it was that he was working at home on his own schedule these days. He still hadn't gotten used to the "on sabbatical" idea, but it was growing on him.

He checked his email, deleted most of it without reading it, and paused. There was a message from Albert.

"Two tickets to Sibelius concert. Want to join me? EOM" That was lawyer speak for End of Message and it always made Larry snort with laughter.

He had once told Albert it felt like a reprimand from a kindergarten teacher, or a prompt from the test proctors. "Do not turn the page until you are instructed to do so." They always had a good laugh about it.

Larry replied to the email. "Sure. Give me a call. All best, Larry." His phone rang almost immediately.

"Hi Larry, hope you are well. My wife is otherwise occupied with some charity thing this Friday, and I thought you might want to join me for the concert. I'll pick you up about 5:30?"

Larry thought Albert sounded exhausted, but he couldn't be sure. "That would be great, Albert. I hope you are doing well."

"As well as can be expected under the circumstances, Larry. I think the concert will be a breath of fresh air. I'm looking forward to it. See you on Friday." The phone clicked off before Larry could reply. Albert was always brusque on the phone and on campus.

Over the years, he and Larry had gone to many concerts and once away from the Institution, Larry found Albert to be charming and even funny at times. He added the concert to his calendar. Not that he had any possible conflict or anything; it was just a long-standing habit.

The next day he told Sara "I'm going to a Sibelius concert on Friday with a colleague, it should be fun. Has your symphony performed much of his work? I particularly like the Violin Concerto in D minor, opus 47, it's so beautifully complex."

Sara's voice was unusually tight when she replied. "That sounds like fun, Larry. Is she, um, is she pretty?"

"What? Who? Is who pretty?" Larry felt his mouth go

dry. What had he said to upset her?

"Your colleague, Larry, is she pretty?" Sara was crying.

"Albert? My colleague is a portly lawyer who bulldozes people into bowing to the will of the Institution Sara, I wouldn't say, and I can't think of anybody who would refer to Albert as pretty." Larry was confused, and a little hurt.

"I'm so sorry, Larry." Sara continued through her tears "My husband was seeing a colleague. A very pretty colleague. We had discussed separating but decided to stay together until my son was out on his own, away at college. At the time of the accident, I felt so guilty because I had actually wished something would happen to him, I was so angry with him, and then when they were killed, I felt like I caused it somehow. Like I was responsible. I'll understand if you think I am a terrible person Larry."

Larry tried to keep it light, but he felt his head begin to pound. "I don't think you are a terrible person, Sara. Far from it. I'm sure we all wish awful things on people when they hurt us. It is just part of being human. You don't have to worry about my relationship with Albert though. We're friends, and we both like classical music."

Sara was still crying, but a little lighter now. "I'm sorry, Larry. I'd better pull myself together and get back to work. Will you still call me tomorrow? I don't know what I would do without these phone calls."

Larry tried to sound cheerful "Of course, same time tomorrow Sara. Bye for now." He hung up the phone and put his head in his hands.

How would he ever tell her the horrible things he had wished on Melinda over the years? Would he ever tell her the story? He thought maybe when they were at dinner, in person, when he saw her in Maryland. That would be the worst possible time though, wouldn't it? To finally get together after all of these years and then talk about depressing things where people died and other people felt guilty for thinking bad things about them? He sighed.

Perhaps it was time to get out of the house and go to the grocery store and drop off his concert going suit at the dry cleaners. He was really looking forward to the concert, and seeing Albert. He needed to clear his head.

He dropped off the suit and made awkward small talk with the dry cleaner. The son of the original owner was now waiting on him, and always told him how grateful his family was for his continued business. Before going to the grocery store, Larry stopped in at the bookstore.

He asked where he might find the Tolkien books, and the young clerk happily skipped back to the section with him.

"Here you go," she waved her hand dramatically, "a whole shelf full of Elven magic!"

Larry laughed and thanked her. He picked out the first book, The Hobbit, and tried to remember if he had read the whole series in high school when everybody else was carrying them around.

"This ought to be a trip down memory lane," he told the clerk at the checkout. "The last time I read it was well before you were born!"

She smiled. "It's a classic, that's for sure! Do you want to update your frequent reader card? Looks like it has been awhile since you read anything other than deep science. We try to keep our categories full of what people really want to read."

Larry thought for a moment. "No, I'll see how I do with this, and maybe I'll update my interests the next time I come in. Thanks, though."

She nodded and rang up his purchase. "Do you want a bag?"

"Oh no thanks, no bag necessary." said Larry. "Maybe

I'm not saving any trees by reading books printed on paper, but at least by not using a bag I'm…" he suddenly noticed she was frowning at him.

"Next!" she said curtly.

Larry hadn't realized there was a line forming behind him. He sighed. He often felt awkward and tongue-tied in social conversations, and he guessed that was why it had been so refreshing to talk with Sara.

So easy and light mostly, until today. He tried not to go back into the dark mood he had been in when he left the house. He slid the book under his front seat and headed off for the grocery store. He turned on the radio and hummed along to the classical music. He felt his shoulders relax just a little. His jaw was still tightly clenched.

"Ok, Larry," he said out loud, looking at himself in his rear view mirror briefly "snap out of it." He practiced his deep breathing exercises in the parking lot before he went into the store.

He read labels and focused on the list that he had apparently forgotten on the kitchen counter. As he made his way around the store he felt his mood lighten a little.

Their conversation the next day was mostly about books and music. Sara and Larry had lots to talk about if they just stuck to Sibelius and epic quests.

Larry had started reading The Hobbit, a chapter each night before bedtime, and it had brought back so many memories of his own idea of what it was going to be like to go out in the adult world and fight the battles necessary for work.

"It's amazing" he told Sara "I had no idea there would really be the equivalent of fire breathing dragons and riddles to solve…"

"Oh I know, Larry. It all seemed like a fairy story then, you know. If we could just get back to the simpler times and keep those greedy people from ruining it all." Sara sighed. "Enjoy the concert tonight, Larry. I'll be thinking of you."

"I'll be thinking of you too, Sara. Bye for now." Larry set the phone down and leaned back in his chair, hands behind his head.

He'd forgotten so much of his youthful enthusiasm about a life in science. Perhaps he'd have a second chance at that as a part of the patient advocacy movement.

His phone buzzed with a notification "Pick up suit at dry cleaners" it said. He swiped the notice off of the screen and slid the phone into his pocket.

After retrieving the suit and picking up a few more groceries, he stopped at the gas station to fill up.

There was a couple at the island next to him washing the windows of their car together. They looked like they'd been doing it together for years, an easy rhythm to their system, each of them doing half of the windows, racing to get it done before the pump clicked off.

Larry felt a strange lump in his throat. Would he ever have that chance with Sara? To just do ordinary things together like grocery shopping and washing the car windows? His eyes blurred as he went to get the receipt for his fill up. He reached into his shirt pocket for his handkerchief and wiped his eyes before putting his glasses back on and heading for home.

When he walked through the door, he tried to imagine what Sara would think of his place. It was simple and functional, and it felt like home to him, but what would it be like to show the house to her?

He set the groceries down on the counter and began to put them away. When he was finished he went back out to the car and retrieved his suit. He stripped the plastic covering off and threw it in the recycling bin. He hung the suit on the doorframe in the bedroom to let it air out. He wondered if she would be getting home from work right about now, what rituals she would be going through at the end of the week.

For years, Larry had watched couples he knew grow distant from each other, fight about splitting things up, how to divide their worldly goods, their time with the children. He didn't know too many couples that were still together after many years. He shook his head. That wasn't exactly true. Albert and his wife were still married, as were several other faculty members, but it seemed to Larry that they spent more time trying to be apart than together.

Perhaps this had just been his way of rationalizing his own single status over the years.

His brother had been married twice, the second time seemed to be a better fit, and they had kids and a crazy busy life together. They always invited Larry for the holidays, and sometimes he'd go for an hour or two, but the sheer chaos was overwhelming to him, and he always had a grant to work on or a deadline that excused him early.

He guessed he had just become so used to a solitary life that it felt like a noble pursuit somehow. His epic journey. Unencumbered by the trappings of family life. That's how his brother had described it once.

"You are so lucky Larry. Your life is your own. You can get up when you want, work as many hours as you want to, and not be distracted by all of the things that drive me absolutely bonkers some days. I wouldn't trade places with you, of course, I'd go insane without the circus."

Larry had smiled. "That's true, you always did want to grow up and run away with the circus, didn't you?"

They had been interrupted by a dog running through the room, covered in mud, followed by three or four laughing kids trying to catch it and Larry had been glad at the time that the conversation hadn't continued.

He'd gotten so weary of the endless offers to "fix him up" with somebody's cousin or friends of colleagues, and questions about whether he was he seeing anyone.

Once his parents had passed away it got a little easier, but he still felt like he was letting people down by just living his life as a scientist, trying to solve kidney disease. An outsider. What would it be like to show up at the holidays with Sara? He smiled to himself. That would certainly be interesting.

He started to get ready for the concert. He took out his shoeshine kit and polished his dress shoes until he could almost see his reflection in them. Then he opened the top drawer of his dresser, where he kept all of the hand knit socks he had made for himself. He selected the blue and white striped pair, with the Finnish flags embroidered around the top. Nobody would see them in the dark, but he imagined Sibelius would be pleased.

CHAPTER FOUR

A lbert pulled up in front of the house a few minutes late, as always.

Larry was waiting just outside the front door and waved. He climbed into the passenger side of Albert's large sedan and pulled the door closed.

Albert was already moving forward. "Sorry I'm a few minutes late, pal, I always thinks I am going to show up on time and then it never happens." He pushed a manila envelope across the seat to Larry. "I picked up your mail. There is something in there from the library I thought you would want, and some current journals. I hope you don't mind."

Albert signaled for his turn and floored the car a little harder than necessary for Larry's taste.

Larry unwound the string from the envelope's fastener and looked inside. Plenty of reading material for a couple of weeks. He rewound the fastener and slid the envelope under the seat.

Albert shook his head. "Why do you always do that, Larry? I'd sure as hell forget what I'd put under there and find it months later."

Larry grinned. "It's an old habit, Albert. I always thought my books were my most valuable possessions, and after hearing stories of thieves looking in car windows to see what they could pilfer, I just started putting books and papers under the seat. I won't pretend I haven't forgotten a time or two, but mostly, it is a system that works for me."

Albert looked at him over his glasses. "You look well, Larry, have you lost a few pounds?"

Larry nodded. "This cooking for myself thing is a little haphazard. I got so used to eating in the cafeteria.... how are things, Albert?"

Albert sighed. "I'm happy to say the case has wrapped up, thank goodness. Apparently a neighbor called the cops twice after hearing Melinda threaten to kill Dr. Rodriguez and reported that there were many loud arguments at her apartment, so the cops had justification to establish motive. It's been a nightmare with Clif though; he's really in bad shape. Just between you and me and the lamppost Larry, he's started drinking pretty heavily. I think he'll be gone by the end of the year."

Larry shook his head sadly. "Gone, like retired, you mean, right Albert?"

"No, gone, as in deceased. He's a prime candidate for a stroke, has been for years. We've already discussed contingency plans. Some days I really hate my job, Larry. I just really hate it."

They rode in silence for the next half an hour or so, each lost in their own thoughts.

"Thanks for this, Albert, I am really glad to be getting out to go to the concert. You know how much I love Sibelius." Larry said softly.

"Yeah, no problem pal. I'm just glad to have some company. Susan doesn't really like the group she's representing at the moment, but it is a real feather in her cap, so she's plowing along. Mostly our conversations are about what we might do if we survive until retirement. I never thought my life would be like this at this age, you know Larry? I really thought all of the hard work and, dammit, I'm sorry. How are you doing? Any job prospects yet? I've got a glowing recommendation letter saved on my hard drive. Just waiting to sign and date it for you!"

Larry laughed. "No, Albert, no prospects yet, but I do have some, sort of interesting news."

He started to tell Albert about Sara and their recent conversations. He left out the part about the accident, as he didn't feel like he had her permission to tell that story.

Albert pounded on the wheel. "That's great. Larry, the best news I've heard in a long time. I really hope you get to see each other in Maryland. Please do keep me informed, will you? That's just great news."

He steered the car into the valet parking area and handed the young man his keys, along with a folded up bill. Another tuxedoed young man opened Larry's door.

He nodded his thanks as he and Albert walked up the stairs to the concert hall.

Larry loved this place. It was old fashioned and musty, but the acoustics were excellent.

Albert patted him on the back. "Maybe next year I'll get four tickets Larry."

Larry felt himself blush as they walked to their seats.

The lights dimmed and a young man in a suit walked onto the stage. "Good evening, friends." he said. "At this time I'd like to remind you to turn off all of your devices. If your phone rings during the performance, you will be required to come up on stage and play a bassoon solo. Nobody wants that!"

A ripple of laughter went through the small audience. Glowing screens hovered in the air as they powered down their phones.

Larry checked his, just in case. He had already turned it off.

The lights went all the way down, and a spotlight came up on the conductor. The first part of the program was a series of short pieces by Sibelius. While he enjoyed them, Larry was most looking forward to the symphony after the intermission. He settled back into his seat and let the music wash over him. All too soon, the lights came up for intermission.

As was their custom, Albert and Larry went out to the back garden, where Albert smoked a cigar and Larry tried his best to avoid the smoke. The courtyard was filled with people.

Larry was always amazed at the number of people who still smoked. He'd never started, and considered himself lucky. He had watched his grandfather and then his father die of lung cancer and he appreciated every breath of air he was able to take on his own.

Albert apologized, as he always did. "Thanks for indulging me my nasty habit, Larry. I keep thinking I'm going to have to give it up some day."

Larry looked down at his feet. He was glad he had taken the time to polish and shine his shoes. They were still serviceable after many years of concert attendance. He'd probably have to have them resoled again soon.

Albert finished his cigar and they headed back inside. They stopped at the men's room and made it to their seats just as the intermission was ending.

The young man appeared on stage again to remind them that if they had been checking their devices for emails and such, the offer of a bassoon solo was still good. The screens flickered again and then he said the words Larry had been waiting for; "And now, without further ado, Sibelius' Third Symphony!" There was polite applause.

Larry loved this piece. He let his mind drift to the picturesque scenery of Finland as the piece unfolded. He had assembled a slide show at home of the scenery he felt complemented the score, and because he listened to this piece whenever he needed to be inspired, it felt almost like an anthem to him.

When the folk-like flute part began, he snapped out of

his reverie. He tried to imagine what Sara looked like when she was a child, visiting her grandparents in Finland. He pictured her running through the forest, picking berries and putting them in a small basket. He knew that was probably a fantasy fueled by the many documentaries he had watched about Finland, but he made a mental note to ask her about it.

He remembered the taste of cloudberries picked on an excursion to the northern part of the country. The music began its crescendo, and Larry switched back to his mental imagery of the slide show. Perhaps he would travel there again and take some new pictures to add to the montage. It was an unlikely dream, he knew, but he wasn't ready to give up on it.

Soon the symphony was ending and the audience applauded appreciatively. The lights came up and they all began to file out of the hall. Albert and Larry stopped again at the men's room and then headed out to collect the car.

Albert tipped the valet and Larry nodded to his door opener. They sped away into the darkness.

Larry's mind was still filled with images of lakes and forests.

Albert cleared his throat. "That was fantastic, didn't you think?"

Larry jumped a little, startled. He reached for the envelope under the seat. "Yes, that symphony is one of my favorites. I can't thank you enough."

"Well, if it wasn't for you Larry, I never would have any culture at all. I need to thank you."

Larry wasn't quite sure what to say. Many years ago he had purchased a set of season tickets to the symphony when a fundraiser had called, imploring his support. They needed to raise the funds to restore the old theatre, save it from being turned into a movie metroplex or something like that. Larry had been in the middle of writing a huge grant and had agreed to buy the two tickets just to get the phone call to end. When the tickets came in the mail, he realized he didn't have anyone to go with him.

Albert had been helping him negotiate some patent application requirements with the University office of technology transfer and Larry asked him if he liked classical music. He remembered that Albert had been surprised at the time but agreed to go with him to the first concert of the series. After that, Albert and his wife Susan became ardent supporters of the restoration project and were instrumental in raising the money for the symphony orchestra's Foundation. They were board members now, and had their names on a small brass plaque in the lobby. Albert reviewed all of the legal documents the Foundation needed to get their nonprofit status, and Susan organized events for donors and musicians.

Larry wondered whether the Foundation where Sara worked had the same kind of structure. He smiled. He was really looking forward to talking with her tomorrow and telling her about the performance.

Albert interrupted his train of thought "Larry, I do hope you are actively looking for an opportunity. I can't really say much about it, but the department is in really bad shape, and it would be better if you found something quickly." He was leaning forward, gripping the wheel. "I'm actually looking for something myself. If anything happens to Clif..."

Larry wasn't sure what to say. He finally decided to try to sound cheerful and said "I have some good prospects, Albert. I'm sure Institutions would line up for miles to have you on their staff."

Albert snorted. "Not really Larry. I'm kind of a dinosaur in my field these days. I actually think I'd be better off with an industry advisory position. Let me know if you hear of anything, will you?"

Larry was shocked. He always thought of Albert, with his bulging Rolodex and email contact lists as the most well connected person he knew. "Of course, Albert. Of course. I'll keep my ears open."

They rode the rest of the way to Larry's house in silence.

Larry opened his door. "Thanks again Albert. I really enjoyed it. Give my best to Susan, will you?"

Albert waved. "Will do, pal. Can't wait to meet this girl of yours. Sara, right?"

Larry grinned "Yes, Sara." He walked quickly up to his door and let himself in. He repeated it to himself over and over again as he was getting ready for bed. "Sara, this girl of mine." He fell asleep almost the moment he slid between the sheets and dreamed of forests and cloudberries and the lakes of Finland.

Larry woke up the next morning happier than he remembered being in a very long time.

He sat down at the computer and entered a post on the Facebook page of the advocacy group. "I'll be at the Rare Disease Day conference on February 29th. I look forward to meeting you there. Here is a link to my research and publications. Cheers, Larry."

He pushed enter before he could change his mind. He hated all of the outreach stuff he was supposed to do; it felt like bragging, which he couldn't abide.

He knew it was absolutely unreasonable for someone to just stumble upon his research and say "hey, that's groundbreaking, we'd like to throw money at your project!" but the endless groveling had really taken a toll on him over the years and he was weary of it. He switched off the computer and went to make coffee and breakfast.

He hummed the flute part from the symphony and smiled. It had been a great performance, and he couldn't wait to tell Sara about it.

Once he'd had breakfast and coffee and done the dishes, he changed into shorts and a tee shirt and started his daily walk on the treadmill. It cleared his mind and often he read journal articles while he exercised, killing two birds with one stone.

Today he turned up the pace a little bit, to a light jog. He missed the ease of running in his younger days, but never missed a day of at least a 45-minute walk on the treadmill. He managed to walk briskly for an hour, and then headed off to take a shower and get dressed.

He knew Sara wouldn't know the difference if he called her in sweaty gym clothes, but it mattered to him, to be dressed appropriately. He laughed out loud. When had he turned into that guy who worried about being dressed appropriately for a phone call? It wasn't like an actual date or anything, although he had decided that their conversations were first dates, of a sort.

He hummed happily as he pulled his favorite sweater vest on over his white shirt. He ran a comb through his hair and checked his watch. Still time before their date. He set the alarm and sat down on the couch and opened the envelope from the departmental mail that Albert had brought him. "That was really kind of him," thought Larry. "I'm lucky to have Albert as a friend."

He started reading the journal articles, making notes in the margins as was his custom, and flagged a couple of the pages with sticky notes.

When the alarm went off, it startled him, as he had been completely absorbed in his reading. He set the journal down on the coffee table and dialed Sara's number.

She was cheerful this morning as well, and they had a long discussion about the concert and the Sibelius symphony number three.

"I'm so glad you like that one, Larry, it has always

been one of my favorites. It conjures up the woods and lakes of Finland for me."

Larry gasped. "Really? Oh that's so amazing Sara. I have a slide show that I play along with it; with photos I took when I was there in graduate school. What do you remember about the forests when you visited your grandparents?"

Sara laughed, "I loved the forests, Larry. We had a special place where we went by train to gather cloudberries. The most amazing taste, I've never forgotten it!"

"Yes, yes," said Larry "almost a combination of all the best of the other berries, and that golden yellow color when they are ripe..."

They were both quiet for a moment, lost in their own thoughts.

"Sara, I can't tell you how happy this makes me, talking with you like this. I am really looking forward to seeing you. Three weeks until the conference! I just got my confirmation that all of the travel plans are complete and they've put me up in a nice hotel for a change. I can have a rental car as well."

Sara started to say something and then said quietly "I'm looking forward to it too, Larry. I just hope you aren't disappointed."

"Why on earth would I be disappointed Sara? Meeting a friend for dinner who shares many of my interests and has known me almost forever, what could be disappointing?"

Sara hesitated a long time before answering. Larry could barely hear her she was so quiet. "I wish I were younger, Larry. I wish we hadn't ever been apart."

Larry paused, his mind racing wildly. "Thank you Sara. I don't know what else to say."

"I think I'd better go now, Larry. Same time tomorrow? Bye for now."

Larry put the phone down and started to pick up the journal again. He was too overwhelmed to dive back into the glomerulosclerosis article. He wasn't sure what to do next. He paced around the kitchen island a few times and then a few more. What in the world was he supposed to think? On the one hand, his heart leapt at the idea that Sara wished they'd never been apart. He felt loved by that comment, in a way that he couldn't quite wrap his head around. He knew what she meant, he thought, that if they could just wipe the slate clean and start over back then, they'd both make different decisions and end up here, together.

He heard his father's voice in his head "If wishes were horses, Larry, even paupers would ride. Don't base your life on wishes, son. You have to go out and make it happen."

Larry's shoulders slumped under the weight of what he felt he had failed to produce for his father. He hadn't provided grandchildren, he hadn't been a real doctor, he had moved far away from the family in both emotion and distance.

Larry got back on the treadmill. For once, he didn't change out of his good clothes. He just needed to walk away from these feelings he was having.

He wished there was a setting on the treadmill for Finland. At the moment, he'd like to walk all the way to Finland.

His phone rang in his pocket. He almost tripped on the treadmill trying to switch it off and answer the phone in the same motion.

He hoped Sara was calling him back, but it was a number he didn't recognize. He ignored the call and waited for it to go to voicemail. It was the weekend. He didn't want to talk to the telemarketers who wanted to sell him solar panels or new gutters or get him to donate to some worthy cause. He started to pace around the kitchen island again.

After several minutes, the voicemail alert sounded. He accepted the prompt and listened to the message. He had to listen to it twice more before he believed it.

The Executive Director of the patient advocacy group was delighted to have seen the Facebook post. He had spent some time looking over Larry's research and was excited about meeting with him at the Rare Disease Day conference. Would Larry mind if a representative from an industry partner joined them for lunch?

Larry listened to the message again, this time with a paper and pen, to write down the cell phone number and office numbers. He sat down on the couch.

He dialed Sara's number without thinking. He didn't even allow her to say hello. "Sara, I have great news. I'm having lunch with the Executive Director of the patient advocacy group during the conference in Bethesda and they want to know if it is all right if an industry partner joins us. I haven't gotten back to them yet, but this is the most exciting news I've had besides talking to you, and I wanted you to be the first person I shared it with. I know it is not our usual time to talk but I just, I just had to call you!"

Sara laughed. "Oh Larry, I'm so happy for you. That's truly wonderful news. I can't thank you enough for sharing it with me. I was worried that I scared you earlier."

Larry tried to slow his breathing a little. "Well you surprised me, Sara. I'm not; well I never have been very good at surprises. I thought of many things I should have, or would have liked to say to you. I guess what I really want to say is that whatever has happened between chemistry class and now, we can't change any of it by wishing it to be different. We can only take this opportunity to make the best of what is to be ahead of us. It sounds like we've both been through some things we wish we hadn't, but let's try to make the rest of our lives better. I feel like with you, mine is already better."

Sara laughed again. "Oh Larry, that's the sweetest thing I think anybody has ever said to me. Really, I am so excited about seeing you and our phone calls are just the brightest part of my days, but I've started to realize how lucky I really am. I have a job that I truly enjoy, a roof over my head and something to look forward to. That's so much more than I had before we started talking again. I was just in this awful downward spiral of despair. Thanks for rescuing me, Larry."

Larry hesitated. He'd never thought of himself as a rescuer. "You are more than welcome, Sara. I feel like we've rescued each other somehow. I probably should call this guy back before he changes his mind about meeting me for lunch, but I just wanted to share the news with you."

"Congratulations, Larry, I'm so proud and happy for you. Go ahead and call him back. I'll look forward to hearing all about it tomorrow. Bye for now."

Larry set the phone down and did a little dance around the kitchen island. "She is proud of me!" he thought jubilantly. "I'm not a total failure after all!"

It took him a few minutes to collect himself before he called Mr. Randolph back. They had a pleasant conversation, and made plans to meet for lunch between the scientific sessions at the conference. Larry wrote down all of the pertinent information and thanked him for the call.

"No, thank you, Larry. You are just what we have been looking for. I'll send you some information by email if that is appropriate. Do you have a personal email I can use?"

Larry spelled out the new email he had recently set up and confirmed it as Mr. Randolph read it back to him. "I'll look forward to hearing from you, sir."

Mr. Randolph laughed. "Let's not be so formal Larry, call me Rick. I'm really looking forward to meeting you."

"Okay, Rick." Larry made a note on his piece of paper. "I'm looking forward to it, too."

He hung up the phone and sat back against the cushions of the couch. This was turning out quite well. Quite well indeed. He transferred all of the contact information to both phones and to the desktop. He'd need to remember to call him Rick. He resisted the urge to search for more information about Rick, and decided to take himself out for an early dinner to celebrate. It wasn't past the time to take advantage of the early bird special at the diner, and suddenly he was ravenous.

Larry sat at his usual table in the corner and picked up the menu.

The waitress came over and started to take his order and then said "Oh, Larry! It's been awhile. How are you, dear?"

Larry smiled and put the menu down. "I'm well, thank you. How is your family?"

The waitress took out her phone and showed Larry the latest pictures of her kids in their sports uniforms and their Halloween costumes, the dogs in their Christmas sweaters.

He nodded approvingly at each one. "You've got quite a clan there."

She smiled and flipped her order pad over. "Yep, praise the Lord they are all doing well. Now, what can I bring you? The steak sandwich is our special, but nothing to write home about."

Larry thought for just a moment. "A Caesar salad, heavy on the anchovies and an unsweetened tea."

"Okay, the usual, then. What kind of grant did you get this time?"

Larry smiled. He was awfully predictable, he guessed.

He used to come in here and celebrate his grants with extra anchovies. "Not a grant, exactly, but an opportunity to go to a big conference. I'm pretty excited about it and thought I'd celebrate. Thanks for asking."

She nodded and headed back to the kitchen to put Larry's order in.

He reached into his coat pocket and pulled out his reading glasses and the small book that had come in from the library. He was looking forward to reading it. When he opened it though, his heart sank. It was in Finnish. He'd have to return it to the library and ask for a translation. He put the book back in his pocket and started to put the glasses back as well. They wouldn't quite fit, as if they were caught on something. He pulled the book back out and reached deeper into the pocket. He had folded up a paper, about glomuroscerlosis and forgotten about it. He shook his head. At least he had something to read now while he was waiting for his food. He got through the abstract and then a large bowl appeared on the table.

"I don't know how you eat those bony little things, but enjoy!" the waitress said cheerfully.

Larry folded the paper back up, replaced it and his glasses in his pocket, and put his napkin in his lap. He ate slowly and steadily, thinking about how he might feel when he was having lunch in the NIH cafeteria with Rick and the person from industry.

He wondered if he should bring any of his publications, or just give them the links on a sticky note or something. That seemed silly. Perhaps he would stop at the print shop on the way home and see if he could make some sort of business card.

He finished his salad, gave the waitress a nice tip and waved on his way out the door. "Thanks again, see you soon Lorraine!"

He patted his pocket to make sure the book and his

glasses were there and then drove to the print shop. He was a little surprised that it was still there. They did all manner of things now, packaging and shipping and money orders and notary services, but it was still called The Print Shop, so he guessed he could still get something printed.

The young man looked up from his monitor. "Good day, May I help you?"

Larry hesitated for a moment. "I usually," but the young man interrupted him.

"I bought this place two years ago. I have to tell all the regular customers that Frank retired and moved to Florida. Can I help you?"

Larry was a little taken aback by this change, but took a look around the shop. "I'm hoping to print out a few cards, with my name and a link to my publications for a conference in two weeks. Is that doable?"

"Sure pal, anything's doable. Are you an author?"

"No, I'm a researcher. I'd like to have my name and then Rare Disease Researcher, and then the link to my publications."

"Okay then, here's the form. Fill it out exactly as you would like it to appear and I'll have them for you in a couple of days. You want the standard business card or more like an index card?"

Larry thought the index card sounded like a good idea. He started to fill out the order form. He printed carefully, in block letters. He pulled out his phone to verify the link, and then handed the form back across the counter.

The young man looked at it briefly and rang some numbers into the cash register. "That'll be $10.72."

Larry handed him a ten-dollar bill and fished out the exact change from the coin section of his wallet. He took the receipt and started to head back to the car.

"I'll call you when your order is ready. Have a nice day." the new shop owner called out to him.

Larry was already thinking about how he might work the cards into the lunch conversation, and waved as he went through the door and out to his car. He drove home, lost in thought.

After a long run on the treadmill, he read a chapter of The Hobbit, changed into his pajamas and got into bed. His mind was still racing around so many things. His quest to discover the treasure of a portable external kidney filtration system and how to make it available to patients. How to solve the riddles of the people he'd meet along the way. He tossed and turned and finally fell into a deep sleep.

For the first time in ages, Larry wasn't sure where he was when he woke up. His sleep had been filled with dreams of disasters and not being able to solve riddles and losing the keys to some door that would get him to the next meeting. Maybe it was the anchovies, he thought.

He made himself some hardboiled eggs and some coffee. He paced around the kitchen island for the six minutes the eggs were boiling and then back in the other, counter clockwise direction while they were cooling.

His mind relaxed a little after his second cup of coffee and he peeled the eggs carefully into the compost bucket. He usually did a longer treadmill session on Sundays; it would probably be necessary to clear his mind today. He washed the coffee cup and the pan he had used to boil the eggs and laid them in the dish drainer to dry.

He glanced out the kitchen window and saw that it was looking like a dreary, rainy day. Perfect for a long jog on the treadmill, perhaps he'd finish that journal article today. He went back into the bedroom and changed into his workout clothes.

He folded his pajamas neatly and then thought better of it and tossed them in the washing hamper. They looked like he'd been wrestling something large in his sleep. He laced up his running shoes and walked back out to the treadmill. He set up the journal article on the holder he had attached to the top of the monitor and programmed in his favorite jog. The machine began to hum and Larry felt himself relax. He walked steadily for 45 minutes to warm up and then jogged for an hour. He felt the tension melt away as he read the article and imagined the woodsy path he might be jogging on.

He'd gotten pretty good at the visualizations in his guided meditation group on campus, and he'd miss that if he went to work at industry, he guessed. That was putting the cart way in front of the horse, he knew, but he still wanted to be prepared for what the tradeoffs might be. He slowed to a walk and cooled down for another ten minutes. He felt as if he could run all day, but he knew his knees would complain in this damp weather if he kept going.

He finished the journal article, disappointed that it didn't have anything new or interesting to report, just a repackaging of the grim statistics of the disease. It concluded with the notion that more needed to be understood about the mechanism of the underlying biology. Larry sighed. The usual pitch for the next grant that would surely unlock the mysteries of the kidneys. Not likely.

Larry was firmly in the camp that they were still a generation away from really understanding the complex biological mechanisms, and that the way forward for patients was to mechanically filter the blood before it got to the damaged kidneys, hopefully allowing the body time to repair the damage once it wasn't under so much stress. He'd argued for years that it was no different than the way they treated blood clots with ever increasingly more sophisticated stents. He had his followers, but plenty of detractors, too.

He didn't allow himself to go down that road today,

and took an extra long shower to wash away the remains of the fight in his dreams.

He took his time getting dressed, pulling a cashmere vest that his mother had knit him over one of his favorite shirts.

She had taken the time to include a pocket for his index cards and mechanical pencil that he had always carried in high school.

He wondered if Sara remembered this vest. It had been his lucky charm. He wore it for all of his exams and his presentations. All these years later he still felt like it brought him luck. He dialed Sara's number.

"Hi Larry, what's new?" Sara's voice seemed calmer than the last few conversations.

"Actually, there's a lot that's new." Larry hoped he sounded cheerful. "Remember I told you about the patient advocacy group? I posted my research publications link on their Facebook page, and wouldn't you know, they reached out to me and want to have lunch at the conference."

"Oh Larry, how wonderful! I know it will be so exciting for them to have you on their side. You did call me to tell me about it yesterday, do you remember?"

Larry was surprised, and chagrined. He usually didn't repeat himself like that. "You know, Sara, I was just thinking this morning that the world is such a small one these days. I mean, I ordered a book from the library and it turned out to be in Finnish. I can just imagine that there is some computer somewhere than can just scan it in and spit out a translated version, you know? It's all pretty miraculous."

Sara laughed. "It is indeed miraculous Larry, and I am so grateful for our connection. I guess I should tell you though, I certainly don't think it is just a coincidence. I spent a lot of time searching for a group like that, and I am so thankful they exist these days."

Larry was confused. "A group like which one, Sara? A Finnish language translator?"

"Oh no, Larry, a patient advocacy group. My son Mikka had a rare disease. He was a patient at the NIH for years. One of the reasons I reached out to you to friend you on Facebook is that I consider all of you researchers miracle workers. I really do. I wanted to connect with you and thank you for your work, and then you turned out to be, well, much more than that. I feel a very deep connection to you Larry. I am so looking forward to seeing you again in Bethesda."

Larry's mind was spinning. He started pacing around the kitchen island while he tried to gather his thoughts. "I'm so sorry about your son, Sara."

"Oh, thank you Larry. His death was truly tragic, and I'm not sure I'll ever get over it, but his life was a shining example of what can be accomplished when you keep on trying. In addition to being a kind, compassionate, funny and stubborn young man, he had a rare chromosomal disorder called Phelan-McDermid syndrome. I'll tell you more about all of that another time, but I just wanted to set the record straight. I wondered why you had reached out to me on Facebook after all of these years, and then once we started talking I didn't want to ruin it by saying something silly like "Thank you for your service." At first when I saw that you wanted to be friends, I thought you wanted to hear about my experience as Mikka's Mom with PMD, but I quickly realized you had no idea about any of that, and it was strangely wonderful to connect with you on all of these levels about Finland and music and books and the old days in Chemistry class. I haven't felt like I had much of an individual identity other than being Mikka's Mom for so long, and you've helped me realize that there is still more that I can do with my life.

For me, not just in his memory. I went back to see the grief counselor yesterday and told her about you, Larry. She feels like I have made so much progress, and I have to agree with her. Thank you."

Larry was still pacing around the kitchen counter. "I don't pretend to understand how I got so lucky, Sara. I've had a long run of what I thought was really bad luck, and I really just wanted somebody cheerful to talk to who didn't care about the Impact Factor of the last Journal I published in. I guess I always remember you as the happy person in Chemistry class. I have to thank you as well. Perhaps we can work together and make something wonderful out of our future. If all goes well at the conference, I might have a new job. Would you still think kindly of me if I worked for industry?"

Sara laughed again. "Oh Larry, I don't really care if you decide to move to Lapland and raise reindeer. I just hope we can have the adventure together."

Larry stopped pacing. He ran his hand along his cashmere vest to activate the lucky powers. "That would be the absolute highest and best outcome of the conference, Sara. I'd like that very much. This might seem like a silly question, but do you, I mean can you, read Finnish?"

"A little bit, Larry. I certainly can't speak it anymore. Just a few words of endearment that my Mother hung onto. She was very proud of her English speaking abilities, and my father was completely flummoxed by the Finnish language. I think that is why they got together originally. She helped him through school and to navigate around the countryside when they met."

Larry smiled. "Well, Sara, I guess you'll have the same opportunity with me. I'll certainly need help navigating around the NIH. I've been on lots of conference calls with different working groups over the years, but I've never actually been there. It has been a dream of mine to go. For that matter, it has been a dream of mine to travel to Finland again. Maybe we can make that happen as well. I'm in the mood to dream big, Sara, and I have you to thank for that. We're kind of a mutual appreciation society, right?"

Sara laughed. "Shall we have a secret handshake and all of that? It sounds like such fun. I haven't thought about what having fun would be like in such a long time."

"Me either, Sara. Me either." Larry stroked his vest thoughtfully again. "I was wondering, I mean, I would completely understand if you don't want to, but how would you feel about chatting over Skype? I have it all set up on my work laptop and I use it all the time for that, but, well, would it seem weird? I just really want to see you."

Sara hesitated. "Before yesterday I would have been totally freaked out, Larry. Not by you. Just by the whole idea of getting out of my little cocoon that I've created here. I don't have Skype set up here at home. We use it at the symphony offices to chat with performers sometimes, to give them an idea of what the venue looks like and all of that. I'll ask the IT guy at work what I would need to set it up here at home. I'd really like to see you too, Larry. That's a great idea. I need to run into the office this afternoon to help set up for a special event at the concert hall tonight. I'll look forward to telling you all about it tomorrow. Bye for now!"

Larry sat down on the couch and leaned his head back on the cushions. The vest still had some luck left in it, that's for sure. His mother would probably be thrilled about Sara.

He sat up straight and tried to remember. Had he ever introduced Sara to his Mom? His memory was not clear about those kinds of things. He knew one thing for certain, though. He was going to get a haircut this afternoon and spruce up his office for the Skype call. He took off the vest, folded it carefully and placed it into the cedar chest at the back of his closet. He whistled happily to himself as he pulled on his coat and headed to the barbershop. His good luck streak continued as he found a parking place right in front. He walked into the shop and smiled as the old fashioned bell rang above the door.

Tony looked up from the client he was working on. "Have a seat Larry, only two in front of you today."

Larry took a seat and opened the journal he had brought with him. Before he could get too involved in the article, he looked around the small shop. It hadn't changed a bit since he had started coming here, gosh, how long had it been now?

Larry had looked up barbershops in the yellow pages when he first came out for his interview. He had been impressed with the immaculate way Tony had taken care of his haircutting tools, as if they were surgical instruments.

There were always a couple of young men sweeping the floor and wiping off the chairs and folding towels. Usually they were Tony's nephews, although the newest generation might be his grandchildren or their cousins. The sports news was always on a small television and Larry had always felt welcomed and accepted into this shop. Mechanics and plumbers and business tycoons alike, you sat in the chair that Tony pointed to, and waited your turn.

Tony knew the name of your spouse and your kids and how your business was doing and he'd ask about those things as he surveyed the state of your current haircut. Larry had seen him frown a few times at guys who had obviously gone elsewhere since the last cut.

"What happened here?" he'd exclaim in mock horror, looking at the other customers over his reading glasses. "You think I wouldn't notice? What a train wreck this is. I'll see if I can get you back on track."

Larry had never had to undergo that kind of embar-rassment. He'd been a faithful customer for decades now. He went back to the journal article but just couldn't seem to concentrate. He hoped that Sara wouldn't be disap-pointed when they had their Skype date.

Tony called his name. "Step right up here Larry! How's the research going? You got a girl to tell me about yet?"

Larry laughed. "As a matter of fact, Tony, I do. I'm going to see her for the first time in a long time, longer than I've been coming here, so I need a good haircut."

"A good haircut?" Tony put his hand over his chest and feigned a swoon. "I'll give you a great haircut, Larry, just like always."

Larry settled back into the chair and let Tony work his magic. He listened to the latest updates on the grandkids and the extended family.

"I'm glad you finally got your nose out of a book long enough to meet a girl, Larry That's great news." He wrapped the hot towel around Larry's neck and finished up the cut. "Keep me posted. okay? You can pay my grandson at the register over there, but don't tip him too much. He's getting a taste for what real business is like and I don't want it to go to his head!" Tony laughed and winked at Larry. He called the next customer.

Larry went over to the cash register and paid his bill. Tony still didn't take credit cards, just cash. There wasn't a tip jar. You just handed the money to the young man behind the counter and he asked how much change you wanted and if you needed a receipt. Larry had always tak-en a receipt and put it in the shoebox with all of the other receipts he took to his tax accountant in January. He took a mint out of the candy dish by the register and walked out of the shop with a wave. "Thanks Tony, see you soon!"

Larry pulled out of the parking space and made his way to the grocery store. It was getting easier for him to navigate the store these days.

He unloaded his groceries from the cart, lined them up precisely in the trunk of his car, wrapping a long bungee cord around them to keep them from falling over on the way home. As he was returning his cart to the corral in the parking lot, he heard someone calling his name. He turned around to see the young cashier running towards him, waving the Clinical Kidney Journal. He must have left it by the keypad when he was paying his bill.

"I think this is yours, I thought you'd want it." she said breathlessly. "Are you a doctor?"

"Well sort, of" Larry said carefully "I am a kidney disease researcher."

"Oh that's cool, my grandmother is on dialysis. I drive her to the dialysis center three days a week and wait with her sometimes."

Larry was surprised. "Oh, good for you. Thanks for the journal. My mind must have been elsewhere. Is your Grandmother doing dialysis at home as well? That greatly improves the clinical outcomes."

She nodded and he turned to the car but the young woman kept talking. "How do you get to research kidney disease? Do you have to go to a special school? I'm studying Biology in high school and I really like it."

Larry turned back toward her. "Keep taking biology classes. That's the key to solving most of these diseases. Study the basic biology."

"Oh, okay, thanks. I'd better get back to work now. Keep up the good work Larry!" She ran back toward the store.

Larry stood there for a moment and wondered what she meant. She didn't know what kind of work he was doing. It always puzzled him when people struck up these kinds of conversations. She must have seen his name on the address label, which was how she knew what to call him. Or maybe it displayed on her register when he swiped his rewards card. He shook his head to clear his mind and got into the car.

He put the journal under the front seat. It wasn't like him to forget something like that. Maybe that's what happens when you're in a relationship, when you're in love. He whispered it to himself. "In Love." Was he in love with Sara? He thought it might be true. Even though it had only been a month or so, he and Sara had known each other most of their lives. Had he loved her back then? Larry shook his head again. Perhaps he was just hungry. It was all so confusing.

He tried to focus solely on driving home, but his mind kept wandering back to Sara. He could almost imagine her in the front seat next to him. What would they be chatting about on the way home from the grocery store?

He tried to recall what his parents had talked about when they went to the grocery store. He couldn't remember. Perhaps his mother had gone by herself, or his father had picked up groceries on the way home from the office. He wished he could ask them. There were so many times when he wished he could just pick up the phone and ask his mother the questions he hadn't been able to ask her in the last years of her life.

He sighed with relief when he pulled into his driveway and got the groceries into the house. He put them away and folded the reusable bags neatly and put them next to the front door for the next trip to the store.

He fixed himself some dinner, rinsed the dinner dishes and put them in the dish drainer by the side of the sink. He only ran the dishwasher once a week, when there were enough dishes to make it practical. No sense wasting resources.

He sighed and sat down on the couch to finally finish the journal article.

CHAPTER FIVE

The next day when Larry called Sara, she began to talk rapidly.

"Oh Larry, I could hardly wait to tell you about yesterday. It was so wonderful and beautiful, I almost called you."

Larry smiled. It sounded nice, whatever it was Sara was so excited about.

She continued, "Two of our Board members got married in the concert hall yesterday. They were both widowed and volunteered with the symphony as a way of dealing with their grief, and they found themselves spending more and more time with each other and they finally decided to get married. They shared a love of Beethoven, so the orchestra played the Moonlight Sonata and it was just splendid. Like a fairy tale, Larry. It was so uplifting. I felt like maybe there was going to be a happy ending for all of us, you know? I was really nervous about it because they put me in charge of a lot of the details, and I just didn't think I could handle it. I probably couldn't have a few months ago. I felt like you were there with me Larry, even when they took their vows on stage, I felt like you were there with me."

Larry wasn't sure if she was going to keep talking or if this was a pause where he should say something. "That sounds beautiful Sara, I'm sure you did a great job."

Sara laughed. "Oh, and about the Skype setup, I took care of that too. Our IT guy will come over this weekend and set it up for me. Then it will really be like you are here with me, Larry. Isn't that great?"

Larry nodded. He thought he could wait another week, since he'd waited all these years to see her again. "Yes, that will be great, Sara."

They chatted about the wedding some more, Sara wanted to give him all of the details about what she had been responsible for and how it had all gone off without a hitch. He could almost picture the scene as she described it, although the people were kind of fuzzy and indistinct. He could certainly hear the music in his mind though.

Sara stopped suddenly. "Oh dear, Larry. I am going to have to cut this short. Our Executive Director just pulled up and I was supposed to have something ready for him. I'll look forward to tomorrow. Bye for now."

Larry felt a little guilty, but he was glad to have the time to process all of the information Sara had just presented him with. It was overwhelming for him when people gushed on about things emotionally like she had, and it always took him awhile to take it all in and sort it out.

He wondered if Sara would want to get married in the symphony concert hall. She seemed awfully excited about it. He had trouble sometimes, knowing whether people told him things because they wanted to actually do them, or if they were just brainstorming, or throwing ideas around with no real purpose. He preferred to put ideas on the table when he had a clear actionable plan for actually working on them.

He thought about all of the meetings he'd been in where people had talked about someone working on a project, and what a good idea it was, and when Larry asked what their plans were to follow through on the collaboration, they looked shocked and back pedaled and talked about how it was just a way of stimulating ideas and that they liked thinking about it. Larry tried to avoid working with those people as they made him supremely nervous.

He never knew if they meant what they said, or if they intended to actually do any work or just think about it. It was easier, really, to just work by himself.

This discussion with Sara felt different though. She was excited about something she had worked on and felt that she did a good job. She was happy for the people that found each other and got married, she was happy about the music they chose. It was all very concrete.

Larry liked things that were concrete. It was the emotional, abstract thinking that gave him a headache. He decided he'd better go for a long jog on the treadmill so his brain could sort through all of the parts of their conversation.

He changed into his shorts and tee shirt and chose another journal to read while he pictured himself jogging through the forests of Finland. It wasn't that he didn't have an imagination. It was just that the processing of someone else's emotion and how he should react to it never went very well for him. Perhaps with Sara it would be different.

His mother had always told him that someday he would find someone who loved him just the way he was, as she did. "With unconditional love, dear."

After a long jog and a shower, Larry settled in to work on his presentation for the advocacy group. He practiced addressing Rick. He had no idea who the person from industry would be, so he just inserted "person from industry" as he laid out his strategy. He didn't want to practice that too much for fear he might actually say "person from industry." He certainly could use flash cards to help this process along, and substitute the person's name and title for that card when it came time for it. He organized a set of colored cards and wrote his objectives and salient points on them. Several of the cards, the yellow ones, said "LISTEN, take notes." He sometimes forgot that part and knew it would be important to the success of this meeting.

He was really happy with this system, developed over many frustrating years of feeling completely lost and bulldozed in meetings. When things would get off track he would hold on to his yellow card and make notes. He found that many times these were just diversions, meant to get the meeting off track and simply waste time. Once he could identify the behavior that way, he felt as if the yellow cards held the same significance that they did in soccer games. A warning, for not following the rules, a foul. He never carried any red cards. Green cards were for goals, and white cards were for the facts and data points. Going back to the soccer analogy, he thought he was a good passer, but he was certainly not a goal scorer. That brought too much attention and emotion, things Larry preferred to avoid. They slowed down the process, and often stopped it all together. He shook his head to clear it and pulled out a clean sheet of blank paper. He drew his outline carefully, laying the cards in the appropriate places on the branches. What was he missing? The clock chimed. Ah, dinner.

He left the outline on the coffee table and made himself something to eat. He thought again about the conversation with Sara today. He wondered specifically about the Executive Director. She hadn't seemed afraid of him, more like she shouldn't be on the phone when he was paying her to work there. Larry hoped he had got that part right. He'd ask some more questions about that and try to gauge Sara's reaction and responses for clues.

After he finished his dinner, he rinsed the dishes and put them in the dishwasher with all of the others from the dish drainer. He added the powdered dish detergent and turned the machine on. He waited until the water had heated and began to run through the cycle before heading out the door with the library book. He knew it would be a slow time at the library and perhaps he would get a good parking place at this time of day.

He realized this would be his first trip back on campus since the unpleasantries. That's how he had categorized it, and it kept him calm to think of it that way. There were many unpleasant things in life, and he couldn't dwell on them or his whole life would become unpleasant.

He drove carefully toward the campus. Traffic was streaming calmly, although it was jammed in the other direction.

He smiled. "Good planning Larry," he said to himself out loud. "You don't want to get caught up in that traffic." He pulled in to the parking garage, relieved that his parking sticker still activated the automatic arm to allow him access, and pulled the library book out from under the front seat, looked around so he'd remember where he had parked, and locked the car.

He took his usual route to the library, keeping his head down and striding purposefully. It was chilly out and he was glad for the coat and hat he had chosen before leaving the house. He took off his hat in the vestibule of the library and stuffed it in his pocket. It was nice and warm in the library, such a comforting place. There was something wonderful about the smell of books. He walked back to the reference desk and placed the book on the counter.

"Use the screen to check in, please" The reference librarian was about his age. He guessed the students only worked during the day.

He swiped his ID card and then ran the bar code on the back of the book under the scanner.

The reference librarian looked up. "How can I help you?"

Larry thought for a moment. "Well, when I ordered this book, I didn't realize it was in Finnish. Is there a translation available?"

The reference librarian looked at his screen. "Hmmm, let me check." He typed in a few prompts and shook his head. "Nope. That's the only copy and it came out of the archives, so I'm not sure what we can do here."

Larry sighed.

The librarian brightened a little. "Oh, I have an idea. There is a professor here on campus, Pekka something. He is Finnish, although you'd never guess it except by the name. His English is amazing. Perhaps he's in his office. He often comes in here late to check out books like these. Would you like his contact information?"

Larry nodded. He wondered if it was the same Pekka who ordered the pickled herring on rye at lunch in the cafeteria. "Sure, yes, that would be great."

The librarian picked up the phone and dialed a number. He turned away from Larry and mumbled some things into the handset that Larry could not hear. He thought he heard him say "Are you available now? I'll send him over." The librarian took out a campus map and circled the computer sciences building and wrote the office number in big red letters and numbers for Larry. He ran the book under the scanner again. "I've checked it out to you again for another month, Larry. I hope you and Pekka can figure it out. Good evening to you." He turned back to his screen.

Larry took the book and the map and put his hat back on as he left the library. This would be something to tell Sara about tomorrow for sure. As he walked quickly toward the computer sciences building he was surprised to see so many offices lit up in the buildings around him. Shadowy figures scurried about within, like worker bees in giant hives glowing in the dark. When he'd worked late into the night it never occurred to him that most of the campus did the same. He arrived at the entrance to the computer sciences building, which had recently been renamed after some big donor. Larry didn't recognize the name.

The security guard checked his ID and motioned him through the scanners. So much more like an airport than it used to be.

He showed the map from the librarian to the attendant waiting on the other side of the scanner who walked him to the elevator and pressed the button for him. Larry smiled and thanked him but he was already on his way back to his post.

Larry stepped into the elevator when it arrived and pressed the keypad to get to the third floor. Nothing happened for a second, and Larry squinted at the keypad screen. He held his ID up in front of the keypad and it chimed acceptance. The doors closed and he was whisked upwards. He studied the map and figured out his route. The doors opened and he turned left, went down a long hallway and then right at the T intersection. At the end of that long hallway he found Pekka's office. On the door it said Data Manager. He knocked. He heard shuffling inside and stepped back a little bit

The door opened and a thin wiry man motioned him inside. "Larry, is it?" he said as he took piles of papers and books off of a chair and motioned for Larry to sit down. "I'm Pekka. I understand you have some translation for me."

Larry nodded and took the book out of his jacket pocket. He handed it to Pekka who was already on the other side of the desk. Larry looked around the office. There were books from floor to ceiling, pictures of the Finnish National Hockey teams, piles and piles of paper everywhere. Precariously balanced.

Pekka sat down and motioned for Larry to do the same. He patted his pockets and looked around his desk before finding his reading glasses on the top of his head. He opened the small book and smiled. "Would you like me to read aloud, Larry? It is so rare these days that I get a chance to read Finnish."

"Oh certainly, that would be very generous. I don't want to take up too much of your time, Pekka. It looks like you are very busy."

Pekka looked at him over the reading glasses. "Yes, it does look like I am busy, doesn't it? It scares the students half to death when they first walk in here. I rather enjoy the reaction."

Larry was confused but Pekka had already begun to read the Abstract aloud. The sound of Finnish was beautiful to Larry and brought back many memories for him. He wondered if Sara's mother had read to her aloud in Finnish.

Pekka stopped at the end of the abstract. "This is a publication about the treatment of kidney disease with mechanical intervention other than dialysis. The author is indebted to you, Larry, for your work in the field, but points out that the basic biological mechanisms are poorly understood and need further research. Would you like me to go on?"

Larry sighed, and shook his head. "No, Pekka, the format is likely to be that the introduction spells out the history of the research in the field, with many citations and appreciation for the shoulders of the giants he is about to stand upon, followed by his novel idea, spelled out for most of the book, but what I am really interested in is his conclusion. Would it be too much trouble to translate the conclusion?"

Larry took out a couple of index cards and his mechanical pencil.

Pekka nodded approvingly. "That's an excellent writing instrument Larry. I have quite a collection of those." He flipped through the book until he reached the conclusion. He read it aloud in Finnish, and then stopped. "Well Larry, this young scientist believed, twenty years or so ago, that you were right, and that it was merely a matter of developing a pharmaceutical adjunct to your work that would change the field of kidney disease. He had identified the molecular targets for that work and was beginning to collect data. Did it work out that way?"

Larry shook his head. "There have been hundreds of epic poems about this quest in the twenty years since, Pekka. I think we may be close, but so far nothing effective for patients. Thank you for your time." He started to stand up, but Pekka motioned for him to sit again.

"I'm in no hurry to get back to all of this data I am managing, Larry, it is endless. I'm curious why you wanted to read an epic poem of twenty years ago in the original Finnish. Aren't there many, many citations of such work?"

"Well, yes" said Larry carefully, "but I always like to go back to the source material. There is so much information out there, so much data, that I think it gets corrupted over time. Someone makes an error and someone else repeats it, and it goes on and on and there's a lot of bad science being published. In my humble opinion, of course."

Pekka laughed out loud. "Oh, I admire your honesty Larry. You've just described my job in a nutshell. I've got a fancy title these days, I'm a bioinformatician. There is a small wizardly group of us who really understand what that means. I have to keep up with the latest magic tricks and tools to clean the data and make sure we aren't getting false positives or false negatives or God forbid, assuming that correlation is the same as causation.

Every new class of students brings a shorter and shorter attention span. They don't even read the full paper. They search for keywords or skim using some algorithm they have tweaked for themselves thinking it to be a shortcut. We all know what happens in the epic poetry literature when folks try to take shortcuts. I prescribe the Kalevala regularly to these youngsters when they get arrogant with me. Some of them will figure it out and become real scientists some day. Most of them will end up as plodders or dwarves."

Larry tried to follow along with what Pekka was describing. He made a few notes on his index cards. As he stood up he said "Are you the same Pekka who orders pickled herring on rye in the cafeteria? Maybe we could have lunch together some day."

Pekka laughed again. "That would be a delight, Larry, you have no idea how much I would like that. He tapped on his phone screen. "How about tomorrow? About 2pm? Are you free then?"

Larry took out his phone and turned it on. "Yes, 2pm tomorrow is doable. I'll see you then, Pekka. Thanks again for your time." Larry tapped the reminder into his phone's calendar and stood up.

Pekka was already holding the door open for him. "See you tomorrow Larry."

The door closed quickly behind him and Larry heard shuffling inside the office again. He slowly retraced his path to the elevator and made his way back out to his car.

As he sat down in the driver's seat he realized he'd forgotten the book in Pekka's office. He shook his head. Why was he becoming so forgetful as of late? He banged his fist on the wheel and surprised himself when the horn honked. He backed out of the space a little too fast and zoomed towards home.

The traffic was light and the trip went quickly. Larry's mind was spinning, trying to process all of the information that he thought he had captured. As soon as he got in the door he ran to his desk, pulled a pad of yellow legal paper off the top of the stack and began to write as quickly as he could, everything as it had happened, from the encounter with the librarian, through the security procedures and all of what had transpired in Pekka's office.

He frowned at the missed opportunities. He should have asked about the hockey pictures. He should have not forgotten the book. He should have.... he stopped and turned to a fresh page. At the top he wrote in neat block letters "Questions for Pekka" and numbered the ideas as they came to him. The very last one was "Which translation of the Kalevala would you recommend?" He hoped that Pekka wouldn't think of him as a troll, or a dwarf or a plodder.

He stood up and began to pace around the kitchen island. Clockwise ten times, then counter clockwise another ten times. His brain felt calmer now, and he felt like he had processed most of the evening.

He glanced at the clock on the stove. It was much later than he usually liked to eat anything, but he was suddenly very hungry. He opened one of the lower cabinets and spun the lazy susan around until he found what he was looking for. A tin of herring. He decided not to check the expiration date. He was feeling bold.

He peeled back the top of the tin, drained the oil into the sink and happily ate the fish with his fingers over the sink, smacking his lips. Just the sort of thing Bilbo Baggins would have done, he thought to himself. No plodding around here. He rinsed out the tin carefully and placed it in the recycling bin out in the garage.

He read another chapter of The Hobbit before falling asleep.

When he called Sara the next day, Larry happily described his adventure to her. "I'm going to have lunch with him this afternoon and I think he'll become a friend. Such an interesting guy."

"Oh that's terrific Larry. I'm really happy for you." Sara sounded a little distracted. "I am going to have to cut our conversation short today. I have some workers coming over in a few minutes to bid on the plans for a renovation we are doing here at the concert hall. We have to improve the accessibility of our bathrooms to comply with the building codes and I'm really nervous that it won't be finished in time for our Spring Gala. It is one of our biggest fundraising events and I really want it to be done by then. The Executive Director has tasked me with managing the project. It's a lot of responsibility because of the tension between the advocates of historic preservation in this area and the people from the City who want us to be up to code." She sighed heavily. "I just want it to be perfect, and everybody to be happy."

Larry tried to sound reassuring. "I'm sure you will do a wonderful job Sara. There isn't anything wrong with wanting to strive for perfection, as long as the work gets done. My advisor in graduate school used to say "Perfect is the enemy of done." I didn't like it at all at the time, but over the years I think I'm becoming a recovering perfectionist."

Sara laughed. "Oh that's lovely, Larry. I think I will make that my new motto. Maybe we can have our own secret society, the Association of Recovering Perfectionists. You've really brightened my day, Larry. I hope you have a wonderful lunch with Pekka. I'll look forward to hearing all about it tomorrow. Bye for now."

Larry felt a wave of satisfaction wash over him. Sara really seemed to enjoy his company on the phone. He hoped he could translate that into their in-person meeting in Bethesda.

He gathered his thoughts and reread his notes from his meeting with Pekka. He went over the questions to ask him. He repeated them several times, slowly, out loud. He had always been able to recall information better when it was written down, and over the years he had developed a system for these kinds of encounters. He hoped it would work well for him today.

As he drove to campus, he repeated the questions to himself, in order. It calmed him down to have something to override the chatter in his brain that always started before a social encounter.

He'd learned to think of it as a cranky critic, always bent on derailing him and making him feel bad.

He actually spoke out loud to it. "Thanks for the input, Cranks, I'm really glad you pointed out all of the things that could go wrong with this. You can take a break now." Acknowledging the voice seemed to pacify it somehow.

Larry was grateful for the support he'd had from a counselor in grad school who had reassured him that he wasn't hearing voices, that everybody does a certain amount of self-talk and that unfortunately, the voice was nearly universally critical, especially with people on the creative spectrum.

She was the one who had encouraged him to think of himself as a recovering perfectionist. Together with his advisor, Larry had felt like he had a safety net to fall back on when things got tough.

He blinked as he pulled into the parking garage to try and shift from the past to the present tense. He locked his car and walked quickly to the cafeteria. He checked his watch. Five minutes to two. Perfect timing.

Larry was early for everything and had a paralyzing fear of being late. He felt like it was the ultimate disrespect to not show up on time. He often had to wait for others to arrive, but he didn't mind that nearly as much as racing to get somewhere and the ensuing panic it created. He knew it was only in his head, but it was still awful, and he did his best to calculate how long it took to get somewhere and add a buffer zone for his own comfort. He looked up and saw someone striding across the courtyard toward him.

Pekka looked like he was cross-country skiing the way he glided across the ground with long, purposeful strides. He arrived promptly at a minute before two and shook Larry's hand. "I hope I haven't kept you waiting, Larry" he said as he held the door open for him.

Larry shook his head.

Before he could ask, Pekka held out the book to him. "I'm so glad you left this for me to read, Larry. There are some really important points in this research that I'd like to discuss with you. It actually fits in perfectly with a project I've had in the works. I needed some historical context and lo and behold, you brought it to me."

Larry tried to shift his mental outline to include this new information. Perhaps he had been meant to leave the book for Pekka and it wasn't a sign of impending dementia after all. He grabbed a tray from the stack and collected his utensils as they got into the line. "I'm always happy to collaborate, Pekka. I'm very curious to hear what you are working on."

Pekka glanced around. "Let's just have lunch now, Larry, and perhaps you would have time for a walk after that? I try not to mix business with pleasure."

Larry nodded and ordered his pickled herring on rye.

Pekka said "Make that two, and a side of horseradish for me. Thank you."

They moved along the line and into the register area. Larry had a moment of panic, but his ID card still worked and he headed for the tables by the window. He liked to sit in the far corner with at least one exit clearly in view. Pekka followed him and they sat down.

"I noticed the hockey team photos in your office" Larry said, checking the first of his questions off the list. "Do you play?"

Pekka nodded as he slathered the horseradish on his sandwich. "I grew up on the ice, Larry and it is the one place my mind is just completely at rest. I play with a senior league once a week, have done for years. I'm not the fastest guy out there anymore, but I am still pretty efficient." He took a large bite out of his sandwich.

Larry chewed his herring happily, imagining the ice hockey. He had always enjoyed watching it from a mathematical perspective and figuring out the angles involved.

"It's a non contact league, which makes it really delightful at my age." Pekka continued, "I have never understood all of the ways that people try to work out their frustrations on the ice by banging each other into the boards. If you are after the puck, that's fine, but otherwise it really ruins the flow of the game."

Larry nodded. "How long have you been here in the States, Pekka?" Question number two, check.

Pekka laughed. "I came over here for graduate school and stayed to work on a project and then they offered me a job, and now it has been almost 30 years. Hard to believe, really."

Larry nodded. "What did you come here to do, Pekka?" Question three.

Pekka sighed as he finished another large bite of his sandwich and took a long drink of water. "Well, back then it was statistical analysis. Computers were just starting to be useful tools, but they were huge and unwieldy and you had to be at a University to have access. I was interested in analyzing data and organizing it in a logical fashion…" he paused. "I'm kind of a curmudgeon now, but I do try to keep up with all of the new ways people try to package data. What about you, Larry?"

Larry had finished his sandwich, and took a drink of water before answering. He found it helpful to mirror the other person's behavior to keep the conversation flowing. "I was interested in curing kidney disease, but from a mechanical engineering perspective. I thought about how we changed our oil filters in our cars and how that improved the performance, and applied those principles to the problems of filtering the blood."

Pekka nodded. "I read about some of your work in the book you left behind. It's really sensible, Larry. I admire your approach." He stood up and reached for Larry's tray. "Let me put that away for you."

Larry hesitated. He had a very specific way of ending his meal by putting the tray and the dishes on the conveyor belt that ran to the dishwashing station. "That's okay, I've got it, but thanks. I'm looking forward to a nice long walk."

Pekka shrugged his shoulders and they emptied their trays and exited out through the back door of the cafeteria. Larry tried to match Pekka's long stride. "Let me know if I'm going too fast," said Pekka. "Everybody always complains that I go too fast."

Larry laughed "Okay, fair enough."

They walked quickly out of the main part of the campus and toward the sporting fields. Larry knew there was a track and field stadium out there somewhere, but he had never been.

Pekka led the way and started the timer on his watch as they stepped on to the track surface. They had the place almost to themselves. Just a few walkers with their earbuds in. Pekka settled into a comfortable pace and Larry trotted along beside him.

"So," Pekka began purposefully "as I am sure you are aware, Finland has had a registry for kidney disease since the middle of the sixties."

Larry nodded as Pekka continued.

"They got so good at keeping all of their data clean and

sending it to the European data collectors on time that eventually they took over the registry and now manage an astonishing amount of health data, for all of the citizens of Finland. It isn't just kidney disease of course, they have lots and lots of genomic data, but there is a particular kidney disease of Finnish people, Congenital Finnish Nephrosis, that stands out as a model for how you can manage data efficiently and correctly and actually help patients."

Larry nodded again.

"So one of my tasks, and it is a crazy difficult one, is to try and explain the complexity of scaling up that kind of data collection here in the States where the population is so incredibly diverse and the need for privacy almost perverse."

Larry started to say something but Pekka continued.

"I'm really curious, Larry, have you followed this scientist's work since he wrote that dissertation? It would be very important to my project if the three of us could collaborate somehow. I have a big grant that is about to expire, and I can renew the funds if we could pull this off."

Larry shook his head. "It shouldn't be too hard for me to search the literature and find out where he is and what he is doing, Pekka. I have the time now that I am on sabbatical. I'm going to the NIH for Rare Disease Day shortly, but after that I'd be available for a collaboration."

Pekka smiled. "Thanks, Larry. I really would like to wrap up some of this work I have been doing and spend some time in Finland. It would be extraordinary if he was still working at the University of Helsinki, wouldn't it?"

Larry checked off question four. "I want to get back there too," he said. "I really enjoyed my time there in graduate school."

Pekka's watch beeped. "Oh goodness, time's up. I need to get back to my office for another circuitous conference call about standards. Let's keep in touch, shall we Larry?" He waved to Larry and sprinted across the campus to his office.

Larry did a few more slow laps to cool down and walked at a reasonable pace back to his car. He felt like skipping with joy, but he kept that in check. He couldn't wait to share all of this with Sara.

When he got to the car, he pulled the book out of his pocket and slid it under the seat. On the way home he went over and over the conversation, trying to commit it to memory so he could map it out on his yellow legal pad when he got to his study.

Larry's maps covered most of a page of the yellow legal pads he favored, and were intricately detailed drawings of his thoughts in tree form. He worked long into the night on this particular map. He forgot to eat dinner until it was too late. He didn't like to eat anything after 7pm as it sometimes interfered with his digestion and gave him nightmares. He was glad his snack the night before had not had that effect, but he didn't want to push his luck. When he had written down everything he could think of, he stood up and stretched. He was surprised how stiff his neck was. He put the map on top of the stack and started his bedtime routine.

It was a night filled with odd dreams and several awakenings.

Larry got up the next morning and lectured himself strictly. "No wonder you are stiff and sore, Larry. You know better than that. You are supposed to take a break at least once an hour and stand up and stretch. What good is having an ergonomic specialist advise you if you aren't going to follow through on their expertise and advice?" He shook his head to clear the lecture. "Thanks, Brain. I really appreciate the reminder. I'm going to make coffee now." He wished he hadn't stayed at the mapping so long, but he knew that if he took the recommended breaks he might have forgotten an important detail. Then he wouldn't have slept, worrying about what he had missed, so it was a tradeoff, really.

He set up the coffee machine and began to pace around the kitchen island. He rolled his shoulders and turned his head from side to side to try and relax his neck. When the machine beeped, he slid his cup under the nozzle and pushed the button. He usually limited himself to two cups these days, as it really was starting to contribute to his jitteriness, so he sipped it slowly and relished the bitter taste and the warmth.

He turned on the light in the study and pulled the map off of the top of the stack. He went over it again, committing it to memory. Then he went back to his list of questions from the day before and checked off the first four. He frowned. There were still so many questions. Pekka had said they'd keep in touch though, so he'd have time to ask them.

He took out his tablet of sticky notes and wrote the name of the researcher on it, followed by the note: "Where is he now?" At the bottom of the sticky note he wrote "PRIORITY: High" and made a small box in the lower right hand corner. He put the sticky note up on the wall in the far right hand column.

There were only two other squares in that queue under P=H. One was the Rare Disease Day conference and the other was New Job.

He glanced to the left hand column, the easily doable tasks with low priority. He tried to do one or two of these a day, just to have something to check off and put into the shoebox marked DONE.

The shoeboxes were labeled by month and year and neatly lined up in stacks under his worktable. He decided to pick three tasks today and put the notes across the top of his computer monitor. "Change the HVAC filter," "dust the ceiling fans," and "sort the recycling."

They were all on blue sticky notes which meant they were monthly tasks that he could take out of the rotation once he had done them, copying the information onto a new blue square for the following month. He had used index cards for this system originally, but the sticky notes took up less room and seemed more efficient somehow. He still used the index cards for his work system.

He put some eggs on to boil and took out a tin of sardines. He figured a little extra protein would be a good idea since he'd skipped dinner the night before and added the walk with Pekka to his day. He sipped his coffee and paced around the island for the six minutes the eggs were boiling. He took the small pan off of the stove after cooling for another two minutes, poured the hot water down the sink drain and ran cold water over the eggs. He paced in the counter clockwise direction and then added some ice cubes from the freezer to the eggs and the water and went back into the study to check his email.

He'd unsubscribed from many of the lists that he seemed to be on, but there was still a fair amount of mail to go through. Upcoming conferences, invitations to submit to journals he'd never heard of. He never opened those. He put them right into the trash and deleted the trash basket immediately. It was like that "whack a mole" game. They just kept popping up. What a waste of time.

When he'd gone through the email, Larry went back into the kitchen and peeled two of the eggs. He put the rest back into a container in the refrigerator and wrote the date on the glass container with an erasable marker. He slid the container back onto the shelf and took out the mayonnaise jar. He mashed the eggs with the mayo and then opened the tin of sardines. He carefully drained off the oil, added the sardines to the egg salad, rinsed the tin and put it in the recycling bin. He wiped his hands on a towel hanging over the handle on the stove and put the mayonnaise jar back into the fridge. He checked the calendar on the door as he closed it to see if it was a week for the recycling truck to come by. He smiled as he ate his egg salad concoction. It was comforting to have a schedule.

Next week would be a challenge for him, getting ready for the conference and seeing Sara. He'd need to keep things as calm as possible this week. He rinsed his bowl and his fork and put them in the dish drainer.

He went into the study, plucked the first sticky note off of the monitor and went into the garage to get an HVAC filter. Once he'd removed the old filter and put it in the trash, he installed the new one and replaced the cover. He checked off the box on the sticky note and put it in the February shoebox. After he'd accomplished the first task of the day, he always felt like he could keep going. It was just the getting started part that gave him difficulty.

Larry wondered if Sara had a routine or a system for keeping herself moving forward. He wondered if it would be compatible with his system. He shook his head and warned himself not to worry about things so far in advance. It was never productive, and rarely turned out the way his brain thought it would.

He changed into his workout clothes and got onto the treadmill. He knew if he caught the anxiety just as it was awakening, he could jog until it couldn't keep up with him. He went for a longer jog than usual and felt the tension in his neck slowly relax.

He dusted the ceiling fans and put the microfiber towels into the laundry hamper. On to the next task. He sorted the recycling and checked off the box and deposited the finished sticky notes in the shoebox. He'd gotten all three of his low priority tasks done before 8AM!

"Get the easy stuff out of the way to get the ball rolling!" he thought, and then he'd dive into the research. He was looking forward to following up on the library book and the conversation with Pekka.

He took a shower and got dressed for the day, walked out to the study, turned on the work laptop and logged into the system. He opened up a PubMed page and began to search. He typed in "Antti Koskinen" and added "kidney disease" as a filter.

He chuckled to himself at his own joke. "Filtering kidney disease. HA!"

The page loaded, and he was thrilled to see the long list of publications. He sorted them by date. They seemed to come to an abrupt halt about 10 years ago. He added them to his reading file and switched over to search for Antti on the web. It looked like he'd left academia and joined a startup pharma company in Boston at about the same time the research papers had stopped. Larry made a note on his map and created a sticky note to follow up with Pekka on the information when he got back from Bethesda.

He also followed up on another Antti Koskinen. This one was apparently a coach of the Finnish Olympic snowboarding team and was knitting at the finish line when one of his athletes was competing in the Winter Olympics in Sochi. The snowboarding team and their story had been widely featured on the news and it seemed as if the 2016 Summer Olympics in Rio would reveal the finished scarf that the team knit together as a project. Larry wished he could call his Mother and share this story with her. She would have loved it. He penciled a reminder on a sticky note to ask Sara about whether she had seen this knitting story.

He printed out the publications that seemed relevant to Pekka's interests and sat down on the couch to read them. When the alarm beeped on his phone to call Sara, he jumped. He'd been so engrossed in the papers the time had just slipped by. He got up and went to the bathroom, washed his hands carefully and dialed Sara's number.

She sounded happy when she answered. "Hi, Larry!"

"Hi Sara. How is the renovation going?" He looked at his notes from the last call and made a small mark next to the item about historic renovation in compliance with ADA laws.

"Oh, Larry it's going really well. The contractor actually seems to know what he is doing, and provided references for several other historic projects he's completed. I called the names on the list and they were all really satisfied with his work and even emailed me pictures of their projects. I forwarded those to the Executive Director and he seems pleased, which is the thing I was most worried about. He signed off on the project and everything should start next week. The first phase is just demolition and I won't have to be here for that, so the Executive Director also said I can have two extra days in Bethesda. Isn't that great? I thought I was only going to be able to come up for the one day."

Larry smiled. "Oh that's excellent news, Sara. It seems like all of these things are just falling into place. I had a great lunch meeting with Pekka and he wants to do a collaborative project. It sounds like he has a big grant that he is trying to renew, so it would be ideal to be able to help with that." He checked another item off the list. "I know this is kind of off-topic Sara, but I was wondering, do you knit?" He placed another mark on the list.

Sara giggled. "Oh yes indeed, Larry. I don't know what I'd do without my knitting, actually. It keeps my mind calm when things are chaotic, and my life has been chaotic for so long..." she trailed off.

Larry hoped he hadn't upset her good mood.

"Larry, can I call you right back? The Executive Director just drove up and I need to get him to sign something. It will just be a few minutes, I hope."

"Sure, Sara, take all the time you need."

Larry put the phone down and went back to reading Antti's research. He was trying to read the papers in chronological order so he could get some sense of how Antti's career had progressed.

His phone rang again. He picked it up, expecting Sara to continue where she had left off.

It was Albert instead. "Hi Larry, sorry to bother you, but I'm afraid I have some bad news. Clif had a heart attack this morning and is in the hospital. I'll keep you updated."

Larry felt like he was going to be sick to his stomach. "Oh no, Albert. Is there anything I can do?"

"Not really, pal. Just stand by. I'll need somebody to talk to in the next few days. I gotta run."

Larry's phone buzzed with another incoming call. It was Sara. He switched over to her and felt relieved when she told him the Executive Director was gone again, off to do some fundraising, and she happily chatted about the upcoming renovation project. Larry felt himself relax a little, and followed most of the conversation.

Sara was talking about the historically accurate tile manufacturer she had found, and the plasterers who were going to be able to match the wall surfaces, and Larry tried his best to follow along.

"Oh, I'm sorry Larry, I've just been going on and on about the bathrooms. You must be bored to tears. Why did you want to know about the knitting?"

Larry tried to get himself back on track. "I was just reading a story about the Finnish Olympic team and their knitting that made the news. I wished I could share that story with my mother. She was an excellent knitter, Sara, and I've always admired the art. I can knit, but I am mostly interested in the mathematical structure. Does that make any sense to you?" He went on to tell her the details about the Finnish Olympic knitters.

She laughed and said, "Oh Larry, I swear, I think you might be my long lost soul mate!! We'll have to have a long talk about math and knitting when we have dinner in Bethesda. I am SO looking forward to it. I've got to get back to my contractor wrangling at the moment though, bye for now!"

Larry put the phone down and wrote a couple of extra notes on his Bethesda list. "Search for knitting stores near the NIH," "Find the Elizabeth Zimmerman books."

He stood up and began to pace around the kitchen island. He didn't want to upset Sara with the news about Clif. She didn't know who Clif was, and he certainly didn't want to open up the Pandora's box of Melinda and all of that unpleasantness.

He did want to support his friend Albert though, and he tried to figure out what the best way to do that might be.

His stomach started to growl. He made himself a grilled cheese sandwich on rye bread and spooned out a large portion of sauerkraut. He looked out the window as he ate over the sink, leaning forward so as not to get any crumbs or sauerkraut juice on his clothes.

His mind was spinning again. What was the right thing to do when your department chairman had a heart attack? He wished he could call his mother and ask her. He'd have to rely on Albert's direction, he guessed.

He was still hungry when he had finished his lunch, so he decided to take himself out for ice cream. It was a treat he allowed himself every once in awhile when things got overwhelming.

His father had taken him for ice cream to celebrate his academic victories in his younger years, and it was the only time Larry felt like his father had been proud of him.

A trip to the ice cream place might be just the thing.

He slid his phone into his pocket and went out to the garage. He put on his bicycle helmet and his gloves. He didn't bother with the cycling shoes; he was only going into town for ice cream. He pulled on a fleece jacket and took the backpack off of the hook on the wall. Inside were his lock and chain, a water bottle and a tool kit with patches for a flat tire. He wheeled the bicycle out of the side door of the garage, locked it, let himself out through the gate and heard it close behind him with a satisfying click. It had taken him a long time to get that self-closing latch to work just right.

He set off toward town and pedaled hard to try and outrun the anxiety.

His brain kept bringing up the bad stuff. "Clif had a heart attack!"

He countered with "Yes, but that was expected, and Sara thinks we might be soul mates, so that's excellent."

This went on for only a few minutes before the exertion of riding the bike and paying attention to traffic drowned out the battle. Larry felt his shoulders relax and he shifted to a higher gear to up the ante. Powerful pedaling could almost always override his brain's emergency alert system, and ice cream would soothe it even further.

Larry was grateful for the concept of heavy work, having been introduced to it by an occupational therapist in his teens. He was thankful to have survived the turmoil of hormonal induced anxiety, and still used the techniques for what he considered his garden-variety anxiety these days. Anxiety was just a weed in the garden really, but like dandelions, it had its useful properties as well. Larry had found that the anxiety could be used as motivation, almost as fuel to get himself through some of the tedium of paperwork that had been so much a part of his job for so long.

He pulled up in front of the ice cream shop, opened his backpack and locked his bike to the rack. He slung the backpack over his shoulder and walked into the tiny shop. All of the other storefronts on this block and for blocks around it had been bought and sold many times for whatever business franchise was trendy at the time. It was comforting to Larry that there were still 31 flavors, as advertised. He'd only ever gotten one flavor, mint chocolate chip, but he liked the routine of looking at all of the other flavors before settling on his favorite. He ordered a single scoop on a sugar cone and took the cash out of his pocket to pay for it. He put an extra dollar in the tip jar and the teenager behind the counter smiled broadly.

"Thanks, man. I can really use the tips. Saving for college and all that."

Larry nodded and walked outside with his ice cream. He sat on the bench next to the bike rack and slowly ate his treat. His dad would be proud of him for this trip to the Rare Disease Day conference, he felt sure of it. Larry finished his ice cream cone and walked back into the store. He walked to the back, down a narrow hallway and let himself into the men's room to wash his hands. After he opened the door with the paper towel he held the door with his foot and tossed the wadded up paper towel into the trash. He smiled as it went in cleanly. That was a good omen.

He stood a little straighter and went out to get his bicycle. He spun the cylinders on the bike lock and lined up the combination, heard the satisfying click, and pulled the hasp free of the chain. He wound the chain back into three precise loops, relocked the ends together and replaced the system in the backpack. He slid his arms through the straps and swung his leg over the bike.

Looking for traffic, he pulled out into the bike lane and pedaled for home. He made sure to get another round of heavy work in, even though he was feeling fine and especially happy after he had made the paper towel point scoring bonus.

He knew that he had to work constantly to keep the anxiety at bay. It took diligence, and Larry had learned the hard way to be vigilant.

He worked up a good sweat on the way home, taking an extra cool down lap around the block before letting himself in through the back gate. He fished a key out of his fleece jacket pocket, let himself into the side door of the garage and locked it behind him. He had rigged the lights on a motion sensor so that he could put away all of his gear in the proper places. The timer was working perfectly, and the lights in the garage clicked off just as he was entering the house.

He did a couple of pacing laps around the kitchen island to make sure his calves wouldn't cramp up and took a long drink of water from the filtration pitcher in the refrigerator. No sense wasting water to wash a glass that he was drinking water from.

He felt satisfied that he'd been adequately rewarded and got back to reading the papers by Antti Koskinen.

Larry was impressed by his steady progression over the years, and a little embarrassed that his own papers were cited in nearly every one of Antti's. There had been parallel tracks to their research, with Larry's train running on the mechanical side and Antti's running on the medicinal chemistry side. Larry wondered what might have happened if they'd worked in the same lab over the years. Perhaps patients would already have the benefits of their combined ideas by now.

Larry's phone buzzed on the coffee table with a text message from his brother. "Hey, brother, just wondered what you were going to do for your birthday. Always welcome here."

Larry picked up the phone and texted back. "Have time for a call?"

The response came back quickly. "Sure, this is a good time, dial away."

Larry took a deep breath and dialed his brother's number. He explained that he'd be in Bethesda, at the Rare Disease Day conference, but he certainly appreciated the offer. "Thanks Brian, I really do appreciate you remembering my birthday. What's new with you?"

Brian told Larry all about what was going on in their busy family life. His daughter Brianna was in a school musical production and her brother Benjamin was still swimming every morning before school and in the afternoons on the school team. Brian sounded weary. "They are growing up so fast, Larry. They'll be off to college in the next few years and then we'll be empty nesters."

Larry laughed. He tried to figure out a way to tell Brian about Sara, but he just couldn't figure out how to tie that in with the empty nester idea without going into her tragic story.

"Have a great time at the conference Larry. I'm sure you will enjoy it."

Larry nodded. "Thanks Brian, I'm looking forward to it. Talk to you soon, bye for now." He hung up the phone.

He was grateful that Brian reached out to him a couple of times a year so they could stay connected. They'd never been really close, but Larry had promised his mother when she was dying that he'd stay in contact with his younger brother. She probably had told Brian to promise the same thing. She had always hoped they'd be supportive of each other, no matter what happened.

When the estate was settled, and Brian moved his family out to the west coast, he'd told Larry that there was always a place for him at their house, at their table for any holiday, or anytime, really. He had handled all of the details for the sale of their parents' house and brought Larry the furniture and a few other things that Larry had expressed interest in. There hadn't been any bickering or concern over who got what, it was more that they were each so different that it was easy to divide things up.

Larry got all the books and the furniture in the living room and his mother's knitting things.

Brian and his wife were interested in the family pictures and the art work on the walls and arranged to have a sale of the other things to pay for having the house updated to get it ready to sell.

Larry was grateful he didn't have to participate in any of that. He hated those kinds of abstract things, and since Brian was an outgoing salesperson, it fit his personality perfectly. The task of choosing the right realtor probably would have paralyzed Larry and the house would still not be sold. He shook his head to clear that train of thought. He stood up and paced a few more laps, focusing instead on how kind Brian always was to him. He was very lucky to have a brother like Brian.

His phone was ringing now on the coffee table. He ran over to get it, hoping it might be Sara.

It was Albert, instead. "Just wanted to give you an update, pal. Clif is going to have surgery in an hour or so. I'll keep you posted. You doing okay?"

Larry nodded. "Yes, thanks for asking Albert. How about you?"

"Oh, I'm managing, but barely, Larry. It's all very touch and go. I'd better make some more calls. Just wanted you to know the scoop."

"Thanks Albert. Take good care of yourself." Larry hung up the phone.

He didn't want to think of the possibilities. There were lots of good cardiologists and heart surgeons; they'd know what to do. He felt his own heart start to race. He'd never wanted the pressure of being a surgeon. He felt like they were the quarterbacks, the stars of the shows, always needing more attention and applause than the entire supporting cast.

"Different jobs for each of us, according to our abilities" he recited to himself. He needed to get his mind off this track.

He went into the study and fired up the computer. He found the classical station's streaming link and clicked on it. Soon he was happily lost in the music, nodding his head to the melody. He was so grateful for the healing power of music.

He thought about Sara and what it must be like to try and manage the chaos of a renovation in an historic building. He was glad she would be able to get away from that and spend three days in Bethesda.

He pulled up a document on the computer and printed it out. "Checklist and packing list for conferences, version 7.1." He laid it on top of the keyboard and closed his eyes.

Suddenly he was very, very tired. Perhaps he'd read some of The Hobbit and turn in early. He looked at the clock. It wasn't even 5pm yet. He didn't want to get his sleep cycles disrupted right before a trip, that was always a bad idea.

He looked at his lineup of sticky notes. "Clean the bathrooms" the next note read. Useful, productive work. He took the sticky note with him as he went to the hall closet where the cleaning supplies were. He took the basket marked "bathrooms" off of the shelf and unfolded the checklist from inside the basket. He made his way down the list, cleaning the shower, then the toilet, wiping down all of the fixtures. He checked the light bulbs to see if they needed replacing. He moved on to the second bathroom and went through the list again. He put all of the supplies back in the basket, replaced it on the shelf and checked off the box on the sticky note. It was a biweekly task so it went back up on the monitor. He'd have to have two checkmarks on the sticky note before it could go in the "finished" box. He felt better knowing that the bathrooms were clean.

He fixed himself some dinner at 6pm and settled back on the couch to read Dr. Koskinen's papers again.

He was looking for a particular pattern, which almost always didn't reveal itself to him until the second or third reading of the literature. After several hours of reading and note taking and drawing of diagrams, Larry felt like it was a good time to take a break and get ready for bed. He'd read another chapter in The Hobbit and get a good night's sleep.

He put the phone on the charger and turned the ringer and all notifications to silent. He really needed a good night's sleep.

As he settled in to the chapter, he realized it was probably a metaphor for anxiety, the dragon was. He'd have to keep that in mind when he read it the next time. For now he was just going to enjoy it as a children's fairy story.

Larry was grateful that he'd learned to read fiction other than science. The farthest he'd really ventured was into biographical novels, and even then it was disconcerting to him when the emotional states of the characters were placed in the first person. He couldn't quite figure it out, why or how were you supposed to read as if you were inside another character's head? At some point, he figured it was a good way to learn about other people's emotional states and how they really weren't that much different from his own. Even people who seemed to be outgoing and gregarious seemed to suffer from some anxiety. He'd pretended he was an anthropologist, studying a rare and exotic culture. He knew he was the one who was unusual, but he just couldn't normalize himself.

It was so much easier in academia than in the real world. You could be completely obsessed with a single thing your whole career to the exclusion of all else and you were praised, if only occasionally, for being dedicated and focused. Routines were appreciated, practically worshipped in fact.

Going on a quest to take his work to patients, outside the safety of the Institution, where it mattered, that was going to be a very scary undertaking, like the Hobbit's quest. Fighting the battle against kidney disease and time and anxiety.

Larry turned off the night table lamp and drifted off to sleep, dreaming of dragons crashing through laboratories and breaking all of the carefully lined up glassware. He fell into a much deeper slumber then and woke refreshed and inspired. The idea of being on a noble quest felt good.

One needed coffee to prepare for the day's journey, and a nourishing breakfast. Larry hummed to himself as he puttered around the kitchen. He scrambled some eggs in butter and folded in some pickled herring and let some cheese melt over the top. He turned off the burner and let the pan sit for just a minute before he slid the omelet out onto his plate. It was very satisfying when the concoction all stayed together in one piece, but it was delicious regardless. He rinsed his cup and his dish and washed the pan.

"Always use cold water when washing something with protein, to avoid cooking the protein further to the pan," his brain reminded him.

He nodded and rinsed the pan, carefully placing it in the drying rack next to the other dishes. He wiped his hands on the towel and then took another towel off of the top of the refrigerator to replace it. He put the first one in the laundry hamper as he changed into his workout clothes to do his treadmill jog.

He picked up the paper he had been reading the night before, placed it on the monitor of the treadmill and started reading from the beginning again, this time looking for the patterns he had drawn on the diagram. He jogged along, reading carefully and nodding to himself when the structure followed what he expected. He put a small check mark in the upper right hand corner of the document with a small number 2 next to it. He'd be glad later that he'd kept track of the number of times he'd read each of the papers. It was part of his study system.

He took a shower and got dressed for the day. He went in to get his phone off of the charger and was surprised to find he had five voicemail messages. They were all from Albert. He got a fresh yellow legal pad from the stack and put the phone on speaker so he could take notes more easily.

The first message was to let him know that Clif was still in surgery and that Albert was getting worried, as it was taking longer than the surgeons had indicated. "No need to call me back, pal. I just need a place to vent. You are probably already asleep. I'll keep you posted."

Larry wrote down the time of the message, saved it and moved on to the next one. They were all updates about Clif being in surgery, Clif moving to post op, Clif in the ICU again, Clif still in critical condition. Larry had drawn a diagram of the calls, with a little map of where Clif was at each stage.

The last call was very early that morning. Albert sounded completely exhausted. "I'm going to go home and get some sleep, Larry. There isn't any further news. I'll keep you posted. No need to call me back."

Larry appreciated Albert's straightforward style. It was often difficult to know whether to return someone's call when they were just leaving you factual information that didn't seem to require further input. Larry had often been surprised when people angrily asked why he hadn't returned their calls.

He had developed a response that seemed to diffuse most of the situations "I didn't think I had anything further to add."

He made a small question mark at the bottom of the diagram he had drawn and wrote: "uncertain outcome." He left the pad on the coffee table next to the publications, as it was an active conversation. He paced a few dozen times around the kitchen island and took some deep breaths. There wasn't anything further to do but wait for Albert's call. Waiting was not Larry's strong point, but he'd find a way to distract himself until it was time to chat with Sara today.

He went into the garage and looked around until he found the plastic tub he had marked "Mother's Knitting." He pulled it off of the shelf and carried it into the house. He took off the lid and set the tub on the couch next to him. The smell of sheepswool and books was comforting. He took a deep breath. He hoped the Wool Gathering newsletters and the books by Elizabeth Zimmerman were still in the bottom of the tub in the big Ziploc bag he remembered putting them in. He pawed through the yarn and felt the edge of the plastic bag. He felt relieved that he had remembered where they were. He put the plastic bag on top of the wool and reclosed the tub. He left it on the couch.

When he started his packing process for the conference, he would read some of the material to keep him going. Elizabeth's voice had been encouraging to his mother and she had often quoted her sayings to Larry as he was growing up. One of his mother's favorite stories was that she had actually met Elizabeth and had one of her books autographed. Larry thought of Elizabeth Zimmerman in the same vein as Einstein or Edison.

"Unventing" things came naturally to Larry and he loved the term. He never used it around academic scientists of course, but it was his own little conversation with his mother over the years.

Even after she was gone, Larry imagined her asking how his research was going and he'd answer, "Quite well, Mother, I've unvented something to solve that problem I told you about last week."

Larry's mother had always laughed when he'd said that, and it pleased him that she'd been happy about his work. He had asked her about her knitting, and she'd describe something she had unvented following Elizabeth's patterns and they would discuss the math involved. Larry was always astonished that his mother needed to write the math down to solve it.

"Don't you just see the answer in your head and then write it down?" he'd always asked.

"No, Larry, my brain doesn't work the way yours does. I have to do it the slow old fashioned way."

Over the years Larry had accepted the fact that nearly everybody's brain worked differently than his. Most people, even in academia, or maybe especially there, couldn't visualize the outcome of what they were doing. They seemed to plunge blindly down dark hallways feeling their way along until they ended up somewhere totally unexpected. Then they'd say "Aha!" as if their discovery was their intended destination. The only place he'd felt like he was among people who were logical and practical was the time he had spent in Finland.

The Finns seemed to always know where they were in space and time. They'd squint up at the sky if you asked them what time it was, and they knew how long it should take to get somewhere and which way the prevailing winds were blowing. They had read the history of the research they were embarking on and did it with something they called sisu. There wasn't a word in English that directly translated, but it was a determination to succeed against all odds, under any circumstances, for the greater good. Larry loved the word and the concept and often used it as a part of his passwords. Especially when logging on to the submission portals for grants and papers for publications. Larry let his mind wander back to the time in Finland.

He thought about what it might be like to go there with Sara. She could show him the places she remembered, and he could take her to his favorite spots. He went into the study and pulled a purple sticky note out of the drawer. He wrote "Learn Finnish" on it and placed it under the Long Term Goals heading on the whiteboard above his computer monitor. He took out a new piece of yellow legal paper and started a mind map. In the center he drew an oval and wrote "Learn Finnish" neatly inside it. He carefully drew lines, using a metal straightedge from the drawer, radiating out from the center. He let his mind come up with all kinds of ways he might learn Finnish and wrote branched notes off of all of the possibilities he could think of. He colored in the various branches. When he got to the square labeled "Ask Sara", he circled it in purple. He put the map into the standing file he kept on his drawing table and took a break to stretch. He knew that his brain would continue to work on the map as he went through his day doing other things. He'd revisit it again this evening.

He looked at the clock. There was still an hour before it was time to talk with Sara. He looked at his task list and selected the "change the bedding" sticky note and went into the bedroom. He folded the quilt carefully and put it aside. He stripped the sheets and the pillowcases and put them in the laundry hamper. He took them out to the garage and put them in the machine. Then he went to the linen closet in the hallway and got another set of folded flannel linens.

"First in, last out," he said to himself, "things last longer that way."

He hummed as he remade the bed, and sighed happily when he had smoothed out the quilt on the top. He set a timer for the transfer from the washer to the dryer and paced around the kitchen island a few times. He felt an anticipatory sense of dread. The hair on the back of his neck stood up.

CHAPTER SIX

L arry's phone rang.

It was Albert. "He didn't make it, Larry. Clif didn't make it. They tried to do another bypass but it didn't work and he stroked out during the procedure. I'm headed back to the hospital to meet with his family. Just wanted to let you know." Albert was nearly sobbing.

Larry stood perfectly still for a moment and said "What can I do to help, Albert? I'm so sorry."

Albert choked back a sob and then said, "Get a job Larry, as quickly as you can. We all need to get jobs before the department collapses."

Larry nodded. "Okay Albert. Give my regards to the family. My deepest condolences."

"Will do, pal. Sorry for the bad news. I'll talk to you soon." He hung up the phone.

Larry began to pace around the kitchen island. Clif was gone. He didn't really feel anything about Clif, he wasn't actually sorry, because there was nothing he had done to be sorry for, but he knew it had been the right thing to say. He went and got a green sticky note and wrote "Get A Job" on it. He placed it in the high priority lineup, removed the old "New Job" note, and started another mind map. He hadn't gotten very far before the alarm dinged for the transfer of the wash to the dryer.

He put a dryer sheet in with the linens and a couple of rubber dryer balls that were supposed to shorten the drying time and reduce wrinkles. He started back on the map again, but the phone rang, interrupting him. It was Sara!

Larry quickly answered her call. "Is everything all right Sara?"

"Oh yes, everything is fine, I just wanted to let you know that the IT guy is coming tomorrow to set up my Skype here at home and he wants to know what your username is so we can test it. Will tomorrow be a good day for you Larry?"

Larry smiled. "Tomorrow will be splendid, Sara. My username is SisuLarry." There was a long silence on the other end of the phone. Larry checked to see if they had been disconnected.

Finally Sara's voice came back again, wavering a little. "That's astonishing Larry. My username is SaraSisu. Wow. Okay, I am not going to be able to have our usual chat today so I wanted to call you quickly to let you know. I'm hopelessly old fashioned about this, I have the idea from my Mom, of course, that girls shouldn't call boys and all that, but I feel like we are good enough friends where I can call you now. What do you think, Larry?"

Larry stood up a little taller and threw his shoulders back. "I think it is great Sara, absolutely great. Call me anytime you like. I'll look forward to Skyping with you tomorrow."

Sara sighed in relief. "Thank you Larry, I am really looking forward to it. I am a little, well a lot nervous to be honest, but I think it will be comforting to see you! Bye for now."

Larry did an awkward little dance around the coffee table and laughed. He was glad there wasn't anybody around to tell him it was inappropriate to be laughing so soon after the news from Albert about Clif, but he was grateful that he didn't have to have that discussion with Sara. It had all worked out fine.

"As most things do if you don't spend too much time worrying about them." He heard his mother's voice and sat down on the couch again, abruptly.

"Yes, Mother, I suppose they do." He shook his head. Imaginary conversations were not going to help him right now. He needed to start getting ready for tomorrow.

He chanted to himself, quietly, "You only get one chance to make a first impression, after all."

Larry had set up his study so that the background view on Skype looked appropriately scientific. The bookshelves on the wall behind him had been curated so that if someone had taken a screenshot and zoomed in, they'd see that he was up on the latest literature. He had taken to placing a book by the person he was meeting with, if there was one, prominently on the shelf just above his head in the picture. This time he thought it would be good to put The Hobbit there.

He went into the bedroom and retrieved the book, taking the bookmark out and leaving it on the side table. He hoped he would remember which chapter he was on. He took the book to the study and made the switch with the business case study book he'd had there for the last call. He stood in front of the bookcase and squinted a little. The book blended in just fine. He took a duster from the bottom shelf and ran it over all of the books. He checked the electrostatic fluff on the end of the wand. It was time to exchange it for a new one. He dropped the dusty one into the trash basket and went to the cleaning supply closet. He put the empty wand on the shelf next to the box of refills. He'd reload it on his next scheduled dusting day.

Larry wondered what Sara was nervous about. She had said that she had used Skype to show performers the concert hall space, so she was clearly familiar with the technology. Larry shook his head. He needed a distraction. Perhaps a bike ride would be a good idea. He hated to just go out without a purposeful destination. He paced around the kitchen island a few times and tried to think of a reasonable response to Albert's call with the bad news. He could go and get a sympathy card. That would be appropriate under the circumstances. He could ask Albert where to send it when he called again the next time to update him.

Larry felt better now that he had set his destination. The card store had been in town a long time, and Larry felt comfortable there. The sections were clearly marked so you wouldn't get the wrong card for the wrong occasion. Larry liked that kind of order.

He went through his routine to get ready to go for a bike ride and slipped two pieces of cardboard into his backpack to keep the card from getting wrinkled on the ride home.

After the latch on the gate clicked closed behind him, Larry took a deep breath and went out for his ride. He was glad that Valentine's Day was over. Perhaps the card store would be quiet and calm. He couldn't imagine there would be a rush on sympathy cards today, but one never knew about that kind of thing.

He shifted into a higher gear and began to push harder on the pedals to quiet his mind. He felt the tension drop away from his shoulders after half an hour or so of riding. He took the long way to avoid the busy intersections and rode in through the back of the loading docks behind the strip mall.

As he rounded the corner to the parking lot, he had just enough room to squeeze by a large SUV parked illegally next to the building. He pulled up in front of the card store and nosed his bicycle into the rack. He locked it and took off his helmet and his gloves, placing them in the backpack.

He walked into the card shop, and nodded to the lady who asked if she could help him. "Sympathy cards?" he said quietly.

"On the back wall in that far corner. Let me know if you can't find what you want."

Larry thanked her and walked toward the back of the store. He read through the choices and eliminated the categories. Not a family member, not a pet, not a friend. Colleague. That was the category he wanted.

He thought he saw red and blue lights flashing out of the corner of his eye, and then he heard sirens getting closer and closer. He went back to reading the cards until he found one that he thought would be suitable for the occasion. He took the card up to the register to pay for it, but the lady was up at the front window of the shop, talking on the phone.

"I don't know, Sandy, but there are several police cars and an ambulance at the side of the building. Check online. I'll lock the door. I've only got one customer right now."

She clicked the handset and turned to Larry. "I'm sorry, but just to be safe, I'm going to lock us in until whatever is going on is over. I can ring you up back here. I called one of the owners of the store next door and she is going to check into it."

Larry felt a small wave of panic start to rise up in his throat. He hoped they wouldn't be locked in here for very long. He handed the card across the counter and waited for her to tell him how much it was going to be.

She looked over his shoulder. "Oh dear, the ambulance is leaving in a big hurry. I hope everyone is alright." She turned back to the transaction.

Larry counted out exact change from the Ziploc bag in his backpack.

She smiled. "That's a good system you have there. Almost nobody carries change anymore."

There was a loud knock on the front door of the shop. Larry jumped and saw that a police officer was there.

"Excuse me, won't you, I hope he'll tell us that we have the all clear." The shopkeeper ran lightly to the front door and unlocked it. She stepped outside to speak with the officer.

Larry stayed behind and slid the card and envelope between the two pieces of cardboard in his backpack. He zipped it up and slung it back over his shoulder, and slid his other arm through the strap.

The shopkeeper was back in the store, but still talking through the open door. "Oh dear, well thank you for keeping us safe, Officer." She waved to Larry. "We have the all clear now, thanks for your business." She motioned to the open door and Larry walked quickly out to the bike rack.

He nodded to the officer who was already talking on his radio and heading back around the corner. Larry did not want to get caught up in whatever was going on over there. It probably had something to do with that illegally parked vehicle.

He really didn't want to change his route, as he liked going back the same way he came, but he took another way home and was glad to arrive safely. After putting away the bike and hanging up his jacket, he took the card out of the backpack. He hung it on the hook with a small label above it printed with neat block letters "cycling backpack, local trips." There was another backpack next to it packed for longer rides. Larry was very happy with this system and thought it worked well.

The dryer beeped. He had forgotten about his laundry. He sighed, and pushed the "bedding" button. The dryer started to turn again. He took the card into the study and put it in the outgoing box of the mailing station he had set up.

He put a yellow sticky note on the computer monitor. "Ask Albert where to send the sympathy card." He drew a small box to check off and then wrote, "Mail the card" with another box. He exhaled deeply. That was done.

He thought about what to do for dinner, and realized he hadn't had lunch. He'd have plenty of time to catch the early bird special, and on Fridays the diner usually had prime rib. After retrieving the linens from the dryer, and making the bed, he put on a suit jacket and whistled. He wondered if Sara would like to go to the diner with him sometime.

When he'd settled into his usual spot in the corner, the waitress came over to take his order.

"You want the special, honey? It's Prime Rib and it's still on the early bird price."

Larry nodded.

"Iced tea with that?"

He nodded again.

"Two times in a row Larry, you get some more good news?"

Larry shook his head. "Bad news, this time, but a fellow has to eat, you know?"

She laughed. "Yes, yes indeed. It seems like a bad day for news. Did you hear about the shooting over at the strip mall on Evergreen? They think it was a gang thing. Never thought this sleepy little town would have that kind of problem, but there you go."

Larry nodded. A shooting. That would explain the police activity and the ambulance. He was glad he had been in the right place at the right time once again.

The waitress was shouting his order to the cook behind the wall. "He likes it rare. Extra horseradish, the good stuff."

Larry smiled. It was comforting to have someone remember what you liked. He rearranged the salt and pepper shakers and lined up his silverware to be evenly spaced away from the edge of the table. He'd forgotten to bring something to read. He took out his mechanical pencil and started drawing absently on his napkin.

When his food arrived he folded the napkin in half and put it into his jacket pocket along with the pencil. "Thank you Lorraine, I really appreciate the extra horseradish."

She smiled. "Well, honey, if you have any crying to do, that'll get you started. Anything else for you right now?"

Larry shook his head and put a fresh napkin in his lap. He picked up the knife and fork.

She turned away and went to greet the next customers at the door. Larry had just started chewing his first bite of Prime Rib when he heard Lorraine say, "Oh he's a regular, a researcher at the University."

Larry looked up, confused. He saw three police officers. They started to walk toward him. He put down his knife and fork.

"Sorry to bother you buddy, didn't I see you at the card shop earlier?"

Larry nodded. He was terrible at recalling faces out of context. Was this the officer he had nodded at before he got back on his bike? Probably so.

The officer continued. "Did you see anything unusual on your way into the card store?"

Larry shook his head and then said "The big SUV was parked illegally, and I had to squeeze around it, but nothing else unusual, no."

The officer pulled a card out of his pocket. "Well, if you think of anything, give me a call. Sorry to interrupt your dinner. How's the prime rib today?"

Larry took the card off of the table and slid it into his jacket pocket. "It's good. If you like horseradish, this place knows how to order the good stuff."

The officer laughed and headed to the bar where his partners were already seated. "Come on guys, might as well order to go. We've got a long night ahead of us."

Larry went back to his meal. He felt safer with the officers in the diner. He started to relax. The officers ordered their food to go and sat chatting quietly at the counter. Every few minutes their radios would crackle and they'd bark some numerical code into the unit. Larry tried to tune it out and just savor his meal. He ate slowly and carefully, dividing up the horseradish proportionate to the amount of meat he was slicing.

Lorraine slid three Styrofoam boxes across the counter to the officers and offered them a bag.

"Oh no thanks, we'll each carry our own. Have a good night."

Larry kept his head down as they left and kept eating. Once he'd reached halfway on both the meat and the horseradish, he crossed his knife and fork on the plate, took a long drink of iced tea and wiped his mouth with his napkin.

Lorraine came over to the table with a pitcher and a to go box. "More tea?" she asked as she put the box on the table with the check on top of it.

"No thanks, Lorraine. I'm satisfied. That was delicious prime rib tonight."

Lorraine smiled and patted Larry on the shoulder. "Glad you liked it, honey. Hope to see you again soon!"

Before Larry could answer, she was off to pour more tea for someone else. Larry left cash for the bill and a nice tip for Lorraine and went to the rest room and washed his hands before heading home.

"Don't forget your to go box" called Lorraine as he was just about to walk out the door.

"Thanks, Lorraine, have a good night." Larry walked back to the table and picked up his lunch for the next day. He took several deep breaths before he got into the car. He put the box on the passenger seat and made sure it was closed securely. He checked again, and then reached under the back of the passenger seat where he always kept a plastic bag for just this kind of thing. He slid the box into the bag and tied the handles into a neat knot. He put the bundle on the floorboard in front of the passenger side seat.

Satisfied, he adjusted his rear view mirror and backed out of the parking place. There was quite a bit of traffic, and Larry was tense and tired by the time he got home.

The down side of going for the Friday evening early bird special was getting caught up in the traffic afterwards. It wasn't big city traffic, but it still made Larry uneasy. He was a cautious driver, and was astonished at the reckless behavior he often witnessed.

He sincerely hoped the self-driving cars were coming soon. He'd be one of the first in line for that new technology. He imagined the luxury of being able to read in the back seat as the cars proceeded in an orderly fashion to pick people up and drop them off at their destinations. No more parking worries, no more anxiety about what the other driver might or might not do. The cars would run like clockwork. Very sensible. He pulled into his driveway and looked up and down the street. Everybody had at least one car in his or her driveway, just sitting there. Imagine if all of the cars were busy all of the time, fully utilized. Much more efficient.

He reached into the passenger side and carefully lifted the bag with the to go box off of the floorboard. He carried the bag into the house, untied the knot and slid the box into the refrigerator. He folded the plastic bag and took it out to the car, replacing it under the passenger side seat. He locked the car, checked the mailbox and carried the mail into the house. He sorted it over the recycling bin, throwing most of it in there. He took the remaining two bills out of their envelopes, put the outside envelopes in the recycling bin and slid the bills into their return envelopes. He then put them in the standing file on his desk, in the numbered slots three days before their due dates. He checked today's numbered box. Empty. He checked the small box on the sticky note marked "Bills" and took off his suit coat. He took the napkin out of the jacket pocket and placed it on the coffee table with his other diagrams about the work of Dr. Koskinen He put the mechanical pencil on his desk in the pencil holder. He wasn't sure what to do with the business card from the Police Officer. He held it for a moment and then reached for a small cigar box on the shelf next to his desk. It had a small label on it marked "Contacts." It was nearly full of business cards. He dropped the new one on the top of the pile and closed the lid. He put the small pin back into the hole, securing it shut. He returned it to the shelf and sighed happily. He liked it when things were in their proper place.

He took his suit jacket and hung it up in the closet, at the back of the line of nearly identical suit jackets. He went back to the couch and read some more of the research, until he was too sleepy to concentrate. He went through his evening routine, went to the study to get The Hobbit and read a few chapters before turning out the light. Tomorrow he'd get to see Sara on Skype. He fell asleep with a smile.

CHAPTER SEVEN

Larry went through his usual routine on Saturday morning, got in a good long jog on the treadmill and got dressed after his shower. He took The Hobbit off of the bedside table and placed it on the bookshelf just above where his head would appear on camera. He paced a few laps around the kitchen island and checked the clock. Almost time. He went into the study, turned on the computer and checked his emails. After deleting most of them and emptying the trash basket on the screen, he pulled up the Skype application and made sure he was logged in and ready. Was she going to call him? He didn't remember how they'd left it. Just then, a call came in. He answered it and sat up straight. He could hear Sara's voice, but only saw an icon on the screen.

"Hi Larry, we are trying to get this worked out. I can see you, can you hear me?" Sara sounded anxious.

Larry waved. "Hi Sara, I can hear you fine, but I only see an icon." Larry tried to look cheerful. He heard typing on the other end and a muffled voice. He guessed it was the IT guy Sara had mentioned The connection was lost, and Larry waited patiently for it to be restored. It happened often with Skype on the first connection with someone, so he was used to it by now. He took his mechanical pencil out of the holder and put it on top of the list he had in front of him in case he got lost in the conversation.

The connection came back again and Larry answered. "Hi Sara, still no video. Can you hear and see me?"

Sara's voice sounded far away "Yes, Larry. I'm so sorry this isn't working properly. We'll try again in a few minutes."

Larry went back to deleting emails and filing others in their folders.

The connection came up again and he answered. This time he could actually see Sara. She was sitting in front of a bookcase, looking slightly nervous.

She patted her hair. "Hi Larry. I think we are connected now. It is so good to finally see you again!"

Larry pressed the keys on his keyboard to take a screenshot as he always did at the beginning of a Skype conversation.

He smiled. "Good to see you too, Sara. We seem to have a library of books between us. I mean not between us, but together."

Sara laughed. "Yes, Larry I know what you mean." She seemed to relax a little and turned away from the camera for a moment.

She spoke to someone outside the frame and thanked them for their help. "Just let yourself out, see you on Monday. Thanks again!"

Sara turned back towards Larry. "So, where were we, Larry?"

Larry looked down at his list. "We were just going to talk about knitting and math, I think that is where we were."

Sara laughed. She pulled something up off of her lap and held it up to the camera.

Larry leaned forward to look. "Oh Sara, what nice work! It is a sock, isn't it? Do you always make them from the top down, or do you sometimes do the toe up method?"

Sara dropped the knitting back into her lap. "It depends on how much yarn I have or if it is a pattern I haven't done before. I'm kind of, um, fussy about the socks matching. I mostly just cannot stand to sit without something to do. Over the last few years I really think knitting has kept me alive. Properly practiced, knitting soothes the troubled spirit."

"And it doesn't hurt the untroubled spirit either." Larry finished the quote famously attributed to Elizabeth Zimmerman. "I have all of the Wool Gathering newsletters and most of EZ's books from my mother," he said, waving toward a section of the bookcases behind him. "My mother actually met her, you know."

Sara's eyes widened. "Really? That's amazing, Larry. I felt like she was a spiritual guide for me as I was finding my way."

Larry looked down at his list "I was thinking Sara, that maybe we could find a knit shop in Bethesda and go look around. Would you like that?"

Sara nodded happily. "Oh gosh Larry, that would be such a treat. I've got my reservations and everything all set. When are you checking in?"

Larry hesitated for a moment. His travel itinerary was in the bedroom with the suitcase. "I'll email you the schedule, Sara. Will that be alright?" He made a note on his list, and then looked back at the screen. "I have to write things down Sara, or they just get away from me."

Sara nodded and held up a list. "Oh, me too, Larry. There is nothing I like better than checking an item off of my list as done." The list was on college ruled lined paper.

Larry felt, well, he wasn't quite sure what he was feeling, but it was safe and comfortable.

They chatted about the town where they grew up in Wisconsin. Neither of them had been back there since their parents had died.

Sara was an only child, so she had the full responsibility for closing everything out of the estate.

Larry told her how grateful he was that Brian had done most of that.

Sara squinted. "I don't remember Brian. Was he in school with us?"

Larry shook his head. "No, Brian is almost a decade younger than I am, Sara. He was just a baby when you and I were in chemistry class."

Sara looked at her list. "When is your birthday Larry? I seem to remember that ours are very close together."

Larry checked one of the items off of his list. "My birthday is the 27th of this month." He saw Sara writing it down.

"Just a day before mine," she said happily, "we were both almost leap year babies. I think it is so auspicious that we are getting together this year, when it is a leap year. It has always been a special day for me. We can celebrate our birthdays together."

They chatted some more, about the past, and what was on their lists, and where they might meet for the conference. They agreed that Sara would text Larry when she got into town since she was driving up from Virginia, and they would make plans from there.

"It's great to see you, Larry. I'm really looking forward to spending a few days with you in Bethesda!" Sara smiled. She seemed much more relaxed than at the beginning of the conversation.

Larry wasn't a very good judge of how people were feeling, but this seemed to be pleasant for both of them. "Me too, Sara. Bye for now!"

They waved to each other and Larry closed the connection.

He leaned back in his chair and smiled. "Hooray for modern technology!" he thought happily. He sat up straight again. They hadn't made a plan for how to connect next. He started to get a little nervous.

His phone buzzed in his pocket. It was a text message from Sara. "Testing, texting. If this is you Larry, Skype tomorrow at noon?"

Larry replied. "It's me alright. See you tomorrow Sara."

After he transferred the screenshot of Sara to her contact information he got up to make himself some lunch. His brain wasn't spinning to try and process this conversation the way it usually did.

He went back over it a few times and thought about all of the ways they were alike. She liked lists! Larry practically did a jig as he opened the refrigerator to retrieve the prime rib. He wasn't that coordinated though, and ended up just sort of hopping on one foot and then the other.

Larry made himself a sandwich with the leftover prime rib, and slathered it with the extra horseradish Lorraine had included in his to go box. He ate over the sink and washed the breadcrumb flakes down the drain when he had finished. He washed his hands and dried them on the towel hanging on the oven door. Then he went back into the study and awakened the laptop from its slumber.

He took a piece of vellum from his flat file and taped it to the screen after he had pulled up the screen shot from his conversation with Sara. He carefully traced the outline of her head and shoulders and then began filling in the features. He needed a way to memorize her face, away from the background of bookshelves so he might be able to recognize her in Bethesda. He'd know her by the sound of her voice, but Larry wanted to make an impression in his mind, the way he was able to do with maps or other visual data, so he could call it up when he wanted to think of her.

He had come up with this system a few years ago, after reading a book called Drawing on the Right Side of the Brain, by Betty Edwards.

He peeled the tape off of the screen, being careful not to tear the vellum. He took the translucent sheet over to the coffee table and laid it down so that Sara seemed to be standing on her head. He then took another piece of paper out of the flat file, this time a smooth piece of drawing paper, and began to draw what he saw in front of him. It was remarkable how much easier it was to do a portrait this way, and Larry liked the process of capturing the details. He laid the piece of drawing paper on the table next to the vellum and closed one eye. They looked identical. He looked through the other eye and was satisfied that he'd reproduced the image, a map really, of Sara's features.

He taped the two drawings to the front of the refrigerator, still in their upside down orientation.

Every time he'd glance at them he would say out loud, "Oh hello, Sara, there you are!" and hopefully by next week he'd have enough of a file developed in his brain to actually recognize her when they met.

He didn't think of his face blindness as a handicap. It was just the way his brain worked. He knew that most people scanned faces in a way that he did not, but he preferred to use that skill for memorizing maps and data sets and other kinds of patterns that seemed more useful to him.

As he got older, people seemed to be more forgiving of his shortcoming.

Often people would say, "Oh, I have a terrible time remembering names, but I never forget a face!" and he would just nod, and realize they hadn't the slightest idea of what he was talking about.

He hoped it wouldn't bother Sara, but he knew there wasn't anything he could do about that, so he started his laps around the kitchen island. Every time he passed the end of the island closest to the refrigerator, he glanced at the drawings and greeted Sara. He knew from experience that the more angles he glanced from, the more three-dimensional the image in his mind would become. A dozen laps in the clockwise direction, a dozen counter-clockwise.

He went back to the laptop and replayed the audio from their Skype conversation with his eyes closed, trying to link up the sound and the image. He found her voice to be soothing and pleasant, except at the beginning when she had clearly been nervous. Once the IT tech had left, she seemed relaxed and happy.

After he had gone over the audio recording a third time, he shut down the laptop and stood up to stretch. He was so thankful for the technology that allowed him to interact with people from a distance. One or two people at a time in person were usually fine, but it depended on so many factors.

Larry was easily overwhelmed by strong smells or background noises that other people just seemed to ignore and be able to concentrate on a conversation in the midst of what often seemed to Larry as a thousand competing channels, all at the same volume. There were exceptions, of course. He was able to go to the symphony, and the movies, and sometimes be in a large group where they were all focused on the same thing.

He sighed. Looking for a job outside of academia was going to be a big challenge for him, but it was the only way to really get his work to the next level. To patients.

As he let his mind wander to all kinds of random destinations, he tried to access the map of Sara's features. It was getting clearer, but he knew he'd need to practice every day before the conference to have it snap into focus as a fully formed image.

He wondered what Sara was doing this afternoon, and tried to picture the rest of her house that was attached to the bookcase in the background of their conversation. He didn't have enough information and made a note on his list of questions to ask about whether she liked living there and how her house was laid out.

He puttered around his house the rest of the afternoon, completing the chores that were on regular Saturday sticky notes and sighed happily when he had checked them all off.

He switched on the classical music station and let his mind relax into the Mozart that was being played. He moved to the couch and began to process the notes he had made about Antti Koskinen's work. He felt like there was something he was missing, perhaps a paper that had not been entered into PubMed. He put a small question mark in pencil on the map he had been drawing and put all of the papers into a manila folder. He cleaned off the coffee table and took the folder to the study where he placed it in the standing file. He checked the section of his bill paying system to see if there was anything that needed attention on today's date, but it was empty.

Larry was not good at unstructured time, and preferred to have his days scheduled from the time he woke up until the time he retired at night. He sat down at the desk and booted up the laptop again. He spent the next few hours searching through the literature for other ways to narrow down his search for the missing piece of the puzzle of Dr. Koskinen's work. He found a few other references, and some citations, but they were not available to him through his laptop.

He'd have to go and see the reference librarian at the University again to see if they were accessible through the University's subscription. He was so frustrated with the closed access of the system; it was just a huge waste of good research if you couldn't read it. Larry tried not to go down that path, and made a note on his list to go see the librarian and request the next level of access.

After dinner, he went through his bedtime routine, went back out to the study to retrieve The Hobbit from the bookshelf, and read a few chapters before turning out the light and going to sleep. It was a restless night, and Larry woke up extra early, less than refreshed.

He knew it was the anticipation of traveling that upset his sleep cycles, but he wished he could break that habit somehow.

He liked to travel, and had discovered fairly early on that scientific conferences were set up in a very predictable fashion, with a map and an agenda and a regular schedule that was very soothing to him. He usually sat in a seat on the edge of the center aisle in the presentation sessions so he could focus on the speaker and their slide deck easily.

Larry thought about the upcoming Rare Disease Day conference and made a note to download the schedule and the maps on Monday, and again once he got to Bethesda, in case there were any last minute updates.

He made himself some coffee and sat down on the couch. He put the coffee cup on a coaster and opened the drawer in the center of the coffee table. He pulled out a small book of crossword puzzles from the New York Times and began to work on the next one in the series. He felt his brain relax as he worked the puzzle, and hummed to himself. This was his usual Sunday morning routine, just shifted a few hours earlier. He decided to do an extra puzzle to fill the time, and refilled his coffee cup. Two cups was his limit, he reminded himself, or he'd be so jittery he would lose even more sleep tonight.

He watched the sun come up through the windows opposite the couch, and was glad for the golden glow instead of the "red sky at morning sailors take warning" option. He started a third puzzle and hummed a little louder. His stomach began to growl, so he put the pencil in the book to mark his place and aligned it with the edge of the coffee table.

It was earlier than he liked to have breakfast, but he put some eggs on to boil. He did laps around the kitchen island and practiced greeting Sara.

He tried on all kinds of voices, from a very deep, almost growly bear voice, to a high-pitched anxious one. That was definitely the wrong choice as it made it sound like he was worried about where she'd been and exclaiming, "Oh THERE you are!" might worry her as well. He went through the range of voices again and settled on one that calmed him and sounded like it might be reasonable.

He set the timer for six minutes and went back the other way around the island, this time greeting Sara consistently in the same voice every time until it felt like it matched the picture. He liked to have the audio and visual tracks aligned. He turned off the stove just before the timer beeped, and turned off the timer as well. He poured out the boiling water, ran cold water over the eggs and added a few ice cubes from the freezer to help the eggs peel more easily.

He had read some reports that said the ease of peeling hard boiled eggs had to do with how recently they had been laid, with fresher eggs being harder to peel, but he liked his system and he was going to stick with it. There was always some study presenting conflicting evidence for almost everything, and he preferred to do his own validation and testing. He solved a few more clues in the crossword puzzle and then peeled two of the eggs and ate them quickly, washing them down with a large glass of filtered water. He put the other eggs in the fridge and went back to his puzzle. When he had completed all of the clues, he folded down the corner of the page and slid the book back into the drawer in the center of the coffee table.

He went back into the bedroom to change into his workout clothes and took his suitcase from the floor of the closet. He laid it on the end of the neatly made bed. He would start his packing for the conference tonight. He unzipped the suitcase and opened it to let it air out. Then he went out to get a folder of things to read while he was on the treadmill.

Today he chose all of the background material he had printed out about the advocacy group and Rick. He'd need to review this material everyday before the conference to feel confident about speaking with them. The folder was marked "Opportunity to finally meet patients, 2016." Larry settled into a quick walk for a warm up and to let his brain focus on the marketing materials from the patient advocacy website.

They seemed to have a couple of events a year to raise funds, a golf tournament and a holiday dinner. Larry tried to get a sense of who Rick really was. He knew from their phone call that Rick was confident and outgoing and from reading the brochure that he was not a scientist.

According to the materials, Rick's sister had died from kidney disease and left two young children, one of whom had kidney disease as well. Rick was determined to honor his sister's "fight" as he described it, and help her young family have a "different outcome."

Larry sighed and turned up the speed on the treadmill a notch. "There isn't a different outcome, none of us gets out of here alive." He said it under his breath.

He remembered a lecture he had been to early in his career given by a representative of the Nephrology Society.

"We aren't here to try and cheat death, we are here to improve the quality of patients' lives for the time they have with us."

At the time Larry had felt inspired by that Quality of

Life statement, and had used those terms when applying for grants along the way.

At some point though, the bean counters and the insurance companies started using the QOL as some kind of buzzword for marketing, with an entirely different meaning. Larry received countless appeals through emails and in his mailbox out by the street to donate to different causes to improve the quality of someone's life. He knew that most of that money would go to the administrators and marketers and very little of it would actually filter down to the research essential to making a real difference in clinical outcomes. He shook his head to keep from going too far down that track.

He wanted to help these patients spend more time living their lives, less time in dialysis, less time waiting for a kidney transplant, and have a better chance of not rejecting that transplant. That was the focus of his work. He could not guarantee that it would truly improve the quality of a person's life the way the marketing campaigns tried to spin it.

He turned up the speed on the treadmill another notch and tried to refocus on reading the material in his folder. He wanted to be open to the idea that Rick and his group were realistic about the disease and the progress the field had made over the last few decades. He hoped they had not fallen prey to some of the shysters and hucksters that sold snake oil to desperate patients and their families. Larry turned the treadmill up to a run. He needed to outrun this train of thought.

He concentrated on Rick's picture, placed upside down in front of him. He committed to memory the shape of his head, the way his ears stood out at slightly awkward angles from his skull, the shape of his forehead in relationship to the chin, the placement of the eyes.

He made a mental map and repeated to himself "Hello,

Rick, it s nice to finally meet you."

He wanted to come across as kind and friendly with Rick, not appear as formal as some often mistook him for. Their phone conversation and the emails that followed had been brief and businesslike. Larry appreciated Rick's directness and hoped he would be that way in person as well.

Larry closed the folder and ran until the timer beeped. He slowed the treadmill gradually until he was in his preferred cool down pace, and hummed to himself until he felt relaxed and calm. He put the folder back on his desk, took a shower and got dressed for the day.

He went in to set up the laptop and noticed that Sara had already tried to reach him on Skype. He quickly signed in and tried to connect, but there was no answer. He thought perhaps Sunday was a busy day for people trying to connect, so he talked himself out of panicking about it. He tried a few more times, and finally the connection was made. Larry could hear Sara, but the video was not working.

Sara said she could hear and see Larry just fine. "Did you want to hang up and try again, Larry?"

Larry shook his head and said, "No, Sara, we have a connection, let's just talk. Perhaps the video will come back again."

Sara laughed happily "OK, Larry, it is good to talk with you! I tried earlier but it didn't look like you were signed on."

"I was probably in the shower when you called, Sara. Was there something specific you wanted to talk about?" Larry looked quickly at his list.

"Oh, yes, Larry" Sara started to speak very quickly. "I'm just getting so excited, and a little nervous if I am honest, about the three days in Bethesda and getting to see you again and going to a yarn store, it just seems to be so perfect and I am feeling like I haven't felt in many years. I have to thank you, Larry. I have so much to be grateful for, and I have been focused on what I lost, and well, I just wanted to thank you. I feel hopeful. Full of hope. I even thought about going to church today, which was one of the reasons I called earlier. I used to really love the Lutheran church services when I was growing up, and after Mikka was born I just didn't, well, I know I probably was welcome, but I didn't feel that way. Do you go to church Larry?"

Larry paused for a moment. "No, Sara. My parents raised me in the Lutheran church as well, and I loved the music most of all, but I never really felt like I fit in with all of the social parts of it. I have been working seven days a week for so many years that I got out of the habit of going to church. It has only been recently, just before my sabbatical, that I took a few weekends off."

Sara plunged right in again. "Well, Larry, that's okay. I mean I don't think it is important for us to do everything the same way or have everything in common. Oh, I am not saying this very well, but I don't have any expectations, Larry. I am just so grateful that we found each other again, and I don't want to imagine where we might be going from here, just enjoy the time we have."

Larry was drawing a diagram as she was talking, and it kept going in a circle. He was very confused by this conversation and would need to process it later, at length. "Okay, Sara. I'm glad you don't have any expectations, I mean, I don't want to try to figure out where this is going either, I just want to reconnect with you in person and have a nice time in Bethesda." He wasn't sure if that was the right thing to say, but he was relieved when he heard Sara laugh again.

"Oh good, Larry. I am so happy to hear you say that. I never thought I would be so excited for a trip to the NIH again, but I really am. It will be good to see you in person."

Larry nodded. "It will be, Sara. I," but before he could finish his sentence, their connection was lost. He tried to call back again but it wouldn't go through. He picked up his phone and dialed her number.

She answered on the first ring. "Hi, Larry! I don't know what's going on with Skype today. Thanks for calling back. Where were we?"

Larry paused. He wasn't entirely sure where they had been. He looked at his list. "I think you said I should ask you about the knitting." He made a small check mark next to that item on his list.

"Oh, the knitting. I don't know what I would do without the knitting. I usually have a pair of socks on the needles at all times. I've knit a lot of sweaters over the years, and a few blankets, but really, it is just the process of knitting that I find so soothing and comforting. Did you say you know how to knit, Larry?"

Larry was glad they were not on Skype now, as he felt himself blushing. It was kind of a secret, and he didn't really talk about it much. "Yes, Sara. I do know how to knit. I knit a lot of complex ideas into socks or hats or mittens, and then I well, I wear them and it seems to help me work out those complex ideas. Does that seem weird to you?" Larry was perspiring a bit now, like when he got ready to give a talk in a meeting.

"No, Larry, I don't think that is weird at all. In fact I think there is a kind of brilliance in that. I'd love to see some of your work. Will you bring one of your pieces to Bethesda?"

Larry exhaled deeply. "Sure, Sara. I'm guessing it could be pretty cold in February in Bethesda, so I'll bring one of my thinking caps."

He made a note on the packing list and relaxed a little.

"Sara, I'm not really sure what kind of expectations you are worried about, but I guess I have to tell you that I'm not really good at that kind of thing. I'm usually pretty overwhelmed at conferences, and I try to do some of the social activities, but I never really quite get it. I hope you won't be disappointed. I just want you to understand I really do want to see you."

Sara laughed. "I think we are both nervous and overwhelmed, Larry. I also think it is going to be just fine. I need to start packing and getting things ready, so maybe we can talk at our usual time tomorrow?"

Larry was relieved. "Yes, that would be great Sara. I am going to start packing today too. Bye for now!"

He hung up the phone and went in to the kitchen to pace around the island. He tried to make sense of their conversation, but it felt to him like Sara was just going in circles, coming back to the being nervous part and going around again. He didn't know how to respond to that.

What should he have said? He didn't feel like he was nervous about seeing her in person. He had seen her on Skype, they had been talking on the phone, and he'd known her since they were young. He was confused. Maybe getting his packing started would be a good idea. He needed to get his mind off of the track of expectations.

Larry went into the bedroom with his packing list. He checked off each box as he put the carefully folded items into the suitcase. He opened a cedar chest on the floor of his closet and pulled out a hand knitted hat. It looked at first glance like there was an intricately colored pattern knitted into the fabric, but it was really the title of his PhD thesis. Larry smiled. He hoped Sara would like the hat. After Larry had packed the first layer on his list, he moved the suitcase to a small stand he kept folded at the foot of the bed. He closed the top of the suitcase but did not zip it shut.

He took the list back out to the study and sat down at the laptop again. He replayed their Skype conversation and tried to follow it, to diagram it, to see if he had missed an important clue somewhere. He felt like the connection had not been complete, and maybe Sara had been nervous, but he really didn't understand the expectations part.

He powered the laptop down and went into the kitchen to make himself some lunch. The day hadn't gotten off to a good start, maybe it was just one of those days. Larry sighed. Maybe tomorrow would be better.

Larry and Sara talked on the phone every day that week. The conversations were light and pleasant, and expectations were not mentioned again. Larry was feeling really hopeful. His bag was fully packed now, and all of his travel documents were stacked neatly on top of it. His reservation for the airport shuttle was made, his alarm was set to allow him enough time to shower and get dressed and be ready.

He knew he wouldn't sleep very well, that he would wake up every hour on the hour and check to see if the alarm really was set, but he was excited about the trip.

He didn't tell Sara about the not sleeping part, he just said, "I'm all packed and ready to go tomorrow, so text me when you get to Bethesda, won't you?"

Sara agreed to do that and they wished each other safe travels.

When he hung up the phone, Larry let out a long sigh of relief. He had been worried that she might change her mind at the last minute. He paced around the kitchen island. It still wasn't the last minute, actually. She might get halfway to Bethesda and turn around and go back home. Larry shook his head. That didn't seem likely. They had made plans.

Larry gathered all of his reading material for the plane, added several crossword puzzle books from the center drawer of the coffee table, and put all of it neatly into his carry on bag.

It was a flexible briefcase, more like a doctor's bag, and Larry liked it very much. Larry took it into the bedroom and put it on the stand at the foot of the bed next to the suitcase. He felt ready. He checked the weather and the flight information on his phone. He had set up the text message reminder provided by the airline in case of delays, but it looked like everything was on time and the weather was clear. Larry thought this was a hopeful sign.

"Smooth sailing," he thought to himself "everything is all lined up for this to be a great trip."

He would fly to Bethesda on Saturday, meet with Sara Saturday night and spend the day with her on Sunday. The conference was scheduled for Monday February 29th, a truly rare day, according to the marketing brochure for the conference. Larry didn't think of something that happened every four years as rare, but he understood the appeal behind the message. He hoped the sessions would be interesting, and the lunch meeting with Rick fruitful. All of it seemed like an amazing opportunity to move forward. Larry went for an extra long run on the treadmill to try and wear himself out so he could sleep.

CHAPTER EIGHT

As he expected, Larry slept fitfully. He woke up every few hours, checked that the alarm was still set, and finally got up ten minutes before the alarm would have buzzed. He switched the alarm to the off position, put the phone on the charger and got himself ready to go.

After he had showered and dressed, he packed the phone and its charger, along with the laptop and its charger in the carry on bag and placed his travel documents in the side pocket. He carried everything out to the hallway by the front door and made himself a cup of coffee. He ate the remaining two hard-boiled eggs from the fridge and did a few laps around the kitchen island. He went to the bathroom, checked that the timers for all of the lights were set to the "away" mode, checked that the doors and windows were locked, and put on his wool overcoat and hat. He left his mittens in the pockets of the coat as he wheeled the suitcase out the front door and then put the carry on bag on top. He locked the door behind him as the airport shuttle van pulled up.

He settled into the seat closest to the exit door and thanked the driver for being on time. As they sped away to the airport, Larry went over the checklist in his mind. Satisfied that he had completed everything, he looked out of the van window at the city lights. When the familiar airport scenery came in to view, the horizon was just beginning to lighten.

Larry liked these early morning flights. He felt like

there was less chance of being delayed and people were not chatty this early in the morning. Everybody just wanted to get where they were going. He tipped the shuttle driver on top of the fare and asked for a receipt, which he folded carefully and put into his wallet.

After standing in the curbside check-in line to get his suitcase on the way to his destination and his boarding pass printed, Larry went to the security checkpoint. He placed his overcoat, hat and shoes in one tote, his phone and laptop in another, and the carry on bag plus the items from his pockets and his watch in a third. He was glad he had a system for this part of the check-in process. He went through the scanner, collected all of his items, replaced them in their proper places and slipped his feet back into his shoes. He patted his overcoat pocket to be sure the ticket and boarding pass were still there. His house and car keys were clipped to a carabiner in the carry on bag. His wallet was in his back pocket. He took a deep breath and headed for the gate.

He stopped in the men's rest room and got to the gate just as they were lining up for boarding.

"Perfect timing," he thought.

He handed his boarding pass to the attendant who scanned it under a flashing light.

It turned green and she said, "Have a nice flight."

Larry walked down the jet way and stood in line to be seated for the journey. Once in his designated seat, he took the book of crossword puzzles out of the carry on and slid the bag under the seat in front of him. He turned off the power on his phone and put it in his overcoat pocket along with the ticket and luggage receipt. He was pleased to see that both of the people sitting beside him had already put their earbuds in and were frantically checking their work emails on their phones.

Larry leaned back against the seat headrest and closed

his eyes. He didn't like to make eye contact with all of the people boarding behind him and imagine what they might be doing on this trip. It got his mind completely jumbled, and so he avoided it.

Once the announcements were made by the flight attendants, Larry fastened his seat belt low and tight across his hips, as instructed. He located the nearest exits, reviewed the safety manual and tried to relax for takeoff.

Once they were in the air and the flight attendants told him it was safe to do so, he lowered the seat back tray table in front of him and began to work the crossword puzzles.

His neighbors had their work laptops out and were connected to Wi-Fi. Larry thought this was great technology, but didn't use it, as he was concerned about the extra charges and whether they would be reimbursed as a travel expense now that he was on sabbatical.

When the flight attendant came around, he asked for a can of water and a cup with no ice and continued to work through the clues on the crossword puzzle. After he had completed the first puzzle, he drank his water and put the cup and the can in the trash and recycling bags when the attendant came around again.

Larry went on to the next puzzle and hummed under his breath. Almost everyone around him had headphones on or earbuds in and were staring at screens of one kind or another. Larry was glad not to have to make idle chitchat with anybody and very happy that the turbulence on this flight was minimal. Mostly over the Rocky Mountains as he expected.

When the pilot made the announcement that they were making their final descent into the Ronald Reagan National airport, Larry returned the tray table to its locked position and put the crossword puzzle book back into his carry on bag. He put the mechanical pencil in his coat pocket and checked again to make sure the ticket and the baggage receipt were there.

Once the plane was on the ground, Larry retrieved his carry on bag and stood up with everybody else, waiting his turn to exit the aircraft. He walked up the jet way and checked the signs for baggage claim.

An escalator ride and a long walk felt good to him at this point. He stopped in the men's room just prior to the baggage claim area.

As his bag came around on the carousel, he checked the numbers against his receipt and pulled the bag up to wheel it to the shuttle bus stop. It was considerably colder here in the outside waiting area than it had been when he left this morning, so he pulled the hat and mittens out of his pockets and put them on. He sighed happily. So far, this trip was going off without a hitch. Once he actually got to the hotel he'd believe that he was really here.

He checked his travel documents and pulled out his ticket for the shuttle bus provided by the Bethesda North Marriott Hotel and Conference Center where most of the conference attendees were staying.

Larry hoped it wasn't too fancy, as he only had the suit jacket he was wearing, nothing in the way of formal wear. He usually stayed in the Residence Inn when he travelled because they were always laid out the same way and he knew he'd get a clean comfortable room without all the fuss. He guessed he would see what he'd been missing on this trip. The shuttle bus pulled up.

The driver hopped out and checked his ticket, took the suitcase and placed it on a rack system under the bus, and waved Larry toward the seats.

"Sit anywhere you like, sir, we don't have a full bus today."

Larry took the seat closest to the side exit of the bus and pulled out his crossword puzzle book again.

The driver climbed back into his seat and the bus pulled away from the curb.

Larry alternated between doing his puzzles and looking out the window at the scenery. It looked like it had snowed recently, but the roads were clear and it was a brilliantly sunny day. Larry was pleased to see the good road conditions, and hoped that Sara would have an easy drive up from Richmond.

He had looked on Google maps the day before and thought she might have about a two-hour drive on a Saturday.

As they got closer to Bethesda, Larry's stomach began to growl. He looked around anxiously, but the only other occupants on the bus had earbuds in and were working on their laptops. He'd get something to eat when he got to the hotel.

He knew his phone would automatically adjust the time zone to Eastern Standard Time when he turned it back on, and then he could synchronize his watch with it. So far he was right on time according to the signage in the airports. The traffic was steady but not terribly heavy, as it was a Saturday. Larry finished his second puzzle and decided to put the book away. He could see from the skyline ahead that they were almost there.

The shuttle bus driver navigated the narrow streets and pulled down what looked to Larry like an alley, to a luxurious entrance with a gold revolving door.

Larry took out a tip for the driver from his wallet and retrieved his carry on bag. He waited patiently until the driver had his suitcase out from under the bus. He smiled in the direction of the driver and handed him the tip.

"Thank you, sir, have a nice visit here in Bethesda!" The driver tipped his cap and pointed Larry in the direction of the revolving door.

Larry hesitated for just a moment, letting the door go

around several times to judge the speed at which he should enter it, and sighed with relief when it dumped him out in the warm lobby of the hotel.

He stood there for a moment too long and someone bumped into him from behind.

"Oh, I am so sorry!" the young man said, "I never know how fast I am supposed to go in those things. So sorry." He didn't look at Larry, but continued forward.

Larry fell in behind him, assuming he was going to the check-in desk, too.

A large gentleman in a red coat stepped between them. "May I help you?" He had a deep booming voice and Larry cringed a little.

"I need to check in." Larry mumbled.

The young man who had bumped into him continued quickly ahead down a corridor.

The large gentleman (Larry's mind raced. Was he a footman, a bell cap, what did his red coat signify?) pointed Larry back toward a large desk with a sign next to it that said "Welcome Researchers!"

Larry thanked the gentleman and got in line. He set his carry on bag on top of his suitcase and pulled the hotel documents out of it. He slid the luggage forward with his foot as the line moved rapidly toward the counter. When it was his turn, the young man behind the counter typed in his information and took his documentation.

"I'll need your ID sir, and a credit card for any incidentals. Would you like a cookie? Chocolate chip, just baked."

Larry smiled "Oh, yes please, but I'll save it until after I've had something to eat. What are my choices here in the hotel?" Larry took back his ID and documents after they had been processed.

The clerk handed him a brochure and a room key. "These are your dining choices here in the hotel, sir. Be sure to check in to your room and activate your key. Then you can use it to bill the meals to your room." He circled Larry's room on a hotel map and pointed him toward the elevators. "Enjoy your stay with us!"

Larry wrapped the napkin around the cookie and placed it in his carry on bag. He found his way to the room on the map and swiped the keycard through the door handle.

The green keypad flashed, "ACTIVATED" and Larry rolled his luggage into the room.

He set the suitcase on the folding stand he found in the closet, and put his carry on bag on the bed. He opened the curtains and looked out over the city. He thought he could see the NIH buildings, but he'd have to check a map for reference. He reached into his pocket and turned on his phone.

There were already two texts from Sara. One when she was leaving Richmond, and the other, an hour later, at a halfway point rest stop. Larry checked the time on the phone. She'd be here in another 15 minutes or so if the traffic was still light.

He quickly unpacked his bags, hanging his clothing in the closet and placing his toiletries in the bathroom. He set up the chargers on the small table next to the TV and started to take his laptop out, but his phone buzzed again with a text alert from Sara.

"Just pulling in to the parking garage."

Larry texted a reply. "Go ahead and check in, I'll meet you in the Meritage dining room."

"Wonderful," came the message back from Sara, "I'm really hungry."

Larry smiled and relaxed a little. If he was already seated in the dining room, she would recognize him and come over to greet him. It would save him the worry of scanning all of the faces of the guests coming in. This was working out very well indeed.

Larry took a look at the map on the back of the door to familiarize himself with the exit routes in case there was a fire, and then took a look at the map of Bethesda, showing where the hotel was in relationship to the NIH and how it was oriented. Larry held the map up to his view out the window and let his eyes track the streets until he felt satisfied that he knew where he was.

He grabbed his carry on bag with the laptop and the crossword puzzles and headed downstairs to the restaurant. He placed the Do Not Disturb door hanger on the outside of his door, double checked to make sure he had his room key in his pocket and went down the stairs to make sure he knew how the exit actually worked in case there was an actual emergency.

He walked to the end of a hallway and followed the signs to the lobby.

He asked the large gentleman in the red coat if he could direct him to the Meritage restaurant.

Once at the restaurant, he let the hostess know that he was waiting for a lady friend to meet him, could he sit facing the entrance so he could see her when she arrived?

The hostess smiled and said "Of course, no problem." She led him to a table set for two where he could clearly see the entrance of the restaurant. "Your server will be with you shortly," she said as she set the menus down on the table.

Larry slid his carry on bag under the table next to his feet so nobody would trip over it and was just about to open the menu when a young man appeared, ready to take his order.

"Good afternoon sir, may I bring you a drink while you are waiting for your party?"

Larry nodded and asked for an unsweetened iced tea, no ice and no lemon.

"Certainly sir, it will be my pleasure to serve you to-day. Are you a guest here in the hotel?"

Larry nodded again and the server said "If I can see your room key, I'll put everything on your tab."

Larry fished the key out of his pocket and handed it to him. The server swiped the key through a slot on his clip-board and handed it back to Larry.

"Okay, we're all set. I'll be right back with your drink. Would you like water as well?"

"No thank you." Larry replied. "Just the iced tea will be fine." He reached under the table after the server had gone to the kitchen and pulled out one of the conference brochures. He studied the agenda and looked at the maps on the back. By the time his iced tea arrived, he had most of the map committed to memory. He thanked the server and took a sip of tea. It was good and strong, and un-sweetened, just as he had asked. He went back to the bro-chure to review the times of the sessions. Just then, he saw someone coming toward the table.

"Larry!" she said with a big smile.

He recognized Sara's voice. He stood up quickly and she rushed over and gave him a hug. He was a little stunned, but happy she was so friendly. Larry motioned to the table. "Is this okay, Sara?"

She nodded happily and Larry stepped around to pull her chair out for her. "Oh Larry, how kind of you. I guess chivalry is not dead after all!"

Larry smiled and returned to his seat.

Sara was already putting her napkin in her lap. "Have you already ordered, Larry? I hope I didn't keep you wait-ing!"

Before Larry could answer, the server was back again. He greeted Sara and asked her what she wanted to drink, and if she were also a guest in the hotel.

She handed him her room key and then said, "I'd like

an unsweetened iced tea, please. Would you mind if I just ordered my food now as well?" She opened the menu and looked quickly at the choices. "I'd like the large charred romaine salad with grilled salmon added and an extra side of anchovies."

The server turned to Larry "and for you, sir?"

Larry grinned. "I'll have exactly the same thing. It sounds delicious!"

The server nodded and turned away.

Larry was just about to comment on their menu choices when Sara asked about his trip. "Oh, it was mostly uneventful, which is always good these days. How was your trip, Sara?"

Sara told him that there had been hardly any traffic and the roads were clear, and it went by quickly. "I was really excited to get here and see you, Larry. I am so glad this all worked out." She pulled an index card out of her purse and handed it to Larry. "I also did a little research. There is a knitting store here in town, open from noon to six tomorrow. It is called Second Story Knits."

Larry looked at the card. She had written all of the information neatly, including the hours of operation for Sunday. He slipped it into his jacket pocket. "Thank you Sara. I'm looking forward to going there with you."

Sara's iced tea arrived and she held it up to Larry. "Here's to our birthdays, Larry."

Larry held his iced tea up and clinked the top of her glass with his. "To our birthdays, here in Bethesda." he said cheerfully.

Before they could even start a conversation, two large bowls of salad arrived at the table, with two smaller dishes of anchovies, one for each of them.

Larry put his napkin in his lap and smiled. "Thank you," he said to the server.

Sara said "Oh it looks wonderful, thank you."

The server asked if they needed anything else.

They shook their heads, picked up their forks and began to shred the salmon and mix it in to the salad. They each took the plates of anchovies and dumped the silvery fishes on top.

Sara stopped and laughed. "This is so delightful, Larry. I've never known anyone else who likes anchovies the way I do. Most people turn up their noses. We seem to have a lot in common, don't we?" She started to eat her salad.

Larry nodded, having already put a bite of salmon and anchovies in his mouth. They ate quietly and efficiently about halfway through each of their salads.

Sara raised her hand to get the server's attention. "Could I have a to go box for the other half of my salad?"

Larry asked for one as well, and the server took the bowls back into the kitchen.

"Gosh, I was really hungry, and I only had a couple of hours to drive. You must have been famished, Larry!"

Larry nodded and reached down for his carry on bag. He pulled out his cookie, wrapped in a napkin. "I was, Sara, and I've been looking forward to this!"

Sara laughed until there were tears in her eyes. She pulled her cookie out of her purse, also wrapped in a napkin from the front desk. She held it up toward Larry. "Cheers, my friend."

Larry was relieved to find that she wasn't laughing at him, but rather it seemed, with him, and touched his cookie to hers very lightly to avoid breaking either of them.

The server returned with two boxes, marked HIS and HERS and said "Oh, I was going to ask if you wanted to see a dessert menu, but I see you have started without me. Will there be anything else?"

Larry and Sara shook their heads and happily ate their cookies.

The server came back with two bills for them to sign. Sara put on her reading glasses and reviewed her bill. She carefully added a tip and folded the folio shut. Larry did the same.

The server reappeared and said, "Stay as long as you like. We aren't very busy tonight."

They thanked him and there was an awkward silence.

Sara finally spoke first. "I imagine you have a lot of preparation for your conference to do this evening, so maybe we can just chat for awhile and then retire to our rooms. What time do you usually get up, Larry?"

Larry sighed with relief. "I'm a pretty early riser Sara. I usually hit the hotel gym before I take a shower and get ready for the day. We could meet for breakfast around 8, perhaps?"

Sara smiled. "That would be lovely, Larry. I can't really find the words for how wonderful this is. I am so looking forward to this time here in Bethesda with you."

Larry nodded. "I am too, Sara. I really didn't know what to expect. I don't want you to feel as though you are not important, but I do have to attend the sessions at the conference. Would you like to see the schedule?"

Sara nodded happily.

Larry slid his chair around the table until they could look at the schedule together.

Sara asked lots of intelligent questions about each session, and Larry was delighted.

Just then his phone buzzed in his pocket. A text message from a number his phone recognized as Rick Randolph. "Just arrived, hope to see you Monday for lunch. Rick."

Larry showed it to Sara. "This is the Executive Director of the patient advocacy group that I told you about. Would you excuse me while I reply to him?"

Sara smiled "Of course Larry. Take your time."

Larry sighed happily. He did not like to be rushed. He thought for a moment before replying.

"Looking forward to it. Cheers, Larry."

He turned the phone to Sara. "Do you think that sounds okay, or too chummy? I haven't met him yet."

Sara looked at the text. "I think it sounds friendly, Larry. Just right."

Larry smiled and pushed the send button. He turned off the screen and put the phone back in his pocket.

Sara twisted her napkin in her lap. "Larry, I'd like to get my salad back to my room and put it in the refrigerator. Would you be okay with that?"

Larry stood up to pull out her chair. "That would be great, Sara. I'm actually feeling pretty tired. I never sleep much the night before a trip. It is silly, but..." he trailed off.

Sara stood up and hugged him again. "Oh thank goodness Larry. I didn't want to start yawning here at the table and have you think I was bored. This has been so wonderful and I look forward to seeing you in the morning."

"May I walk you to the elevator, Sara? I'm going that way!"

Sara laughed and Larry relaxed. They gathered up their things and walked toward the elevator together.

Larry pushed the up button and when the car arrived, held the door for Sara. He asked her what floor she wanted and pushed the button for her. "I'm just two floors above you, Sara, with a clear view of the city. Do you have a view from your room?"

Sara shook her head. "To be honest Larry, I just put my suitcase on the bed and rushed down to meet you, I didn't even have time to look."

The elevator arrived at her floor and Larry held the door for her. He watched her go down the hall.

She turned to wave at him. "See you in the morning, Larry!"

Larry waved back to her and pushed the button for his floor. He leaned against the back of the elevator and took a deep breath. This was going to work out just fine.

He got into his room and sat down on the bed. His head was spinning. Sara had hugged him, twice, and he hadn't had the usual sensation of wanting to jump out of his skin. She smelled faintly of soap, but had none of the other noxious smells that he found so unbearable.

Larry needed to pace, but there wasn't any space in this hotel room. He changed into his workout clothes and went down to the hotel gym. He was relieved to find he was the only one there. He switched on the treadmill and went for a long run.

He went over their conversation again and again in his mind. It had been pleasant. Larry's shoulders began to relax. He dialed back the treadmill to cool down and completed his workout.

When he got back to his room, he took a quick shower and changed into his pajamas. He set the alarm for the next morning and climbed into bed.

CHAPTER NINE

The next day Larry was up before the alarm, feeling rested and refreshed.

Usually he had a hard time adjusting to a hotel room and didn't sleep well the first night on a trip, but he guessed the long run and the lack of sleep the night before might have contributed to this new development. Perhaps it was just the relief at seeing Sara and not having had a panic attack. He shook his head to clear that thought and went downstairs to the hotel gym.

This time most of the treadmills and cycles were occupied. He was glad to see nearly everybody had headphones or earbuds and most of them were reading or checking their phones.

He got on to a treadmill and set up his workout. Once he had gotten about half an hour into it, he could focus exclusively on his workout, rather than fighting so hard to exclude the noises and smells from the others in the room. At least it got his heart rate up faster, he rationalized. He settled in for a run and reviewed the plans for the day.

He'd have breakfast with Sara at 8AM and they would set their agenda for the day. He liked to know ahead of time what was on the schedule, but he'd learned to set a placeholder so that the anxiety of not knowing would not overtake him. After their pleasant meeting yesterday, he felt more confident that today would be pleasant as well.

Larry finished his workout and put the treadmill in cool down mode. He started to be aware of the others in the room.

He switched the treadmill off and took the stairs back to his room to help himself cool down.

Once in the room he showered and changed.

He checked the local weather on his phone and decided to wear his lucky vest under his suit jacket. He put the thinking hat and mittens into the overcoat pockets and packed the carry on bag with his laptop and maps of the city. He tidied up the room as much as he could, but left the bed unmade for the hotel staff to change the sheets.

He went downstairs to meet Sara for breakfast. He was a few minutes early and found a table. Even before he slid his bag under the table he heard Sara talking to the hostess.

She came across the room quickly, hugging him briefly before he pulled the chair out for her.

"Good morning Larry, how did you sleep? I usually don't sleep well in hotels, but surprisingly I feel like a got a really good night's sleep!"

Larry nodded. "It was the same for me, Sara."

The server came by and poured them coffee and gave them menus.

Larry scanned the items quickly and was just about to order, but the server had already moved on to the next table. He put his menu down.

Sara put hers down as well. "I was thinking about how lucky we are Larry, I mean what are the chances that we would have this opportunity to meet again after all of these years?"

Larry started to do the calculations in his head and then pulled out a pencil to work it out on a napkin.

Sara put her hand on his. "I didn't mean that literally, Larry. I mean, I'd be interested in knowing what the actual chances are, but I just meant that we are really, really lucky, don't you think?"

Larry smiled and put the napkin in his pocket. He'd

figure out the approximate odds later. "Yes, Sara. I'm happy we have this opportunity. I'm not quite sure what to…"

The server came back to take their order and Larry was relieved to switch gears. He ordered smoked salmon and an omelet.

Sara said she thought that sounded delicious and ordered the same. There was an awkward silence after the server left.

Sara spoke first. "That's a beautiful vest, Larry. Is that the one your mother knit for you?"

Larry beamed and told Sara all about the vest. When his mother had knitted it for him and how lucky it was and how he wore it for special occasions. "Like today, Sara. I feel like this is a special occasion."

Sara blushed. "I do too, Larry. I mean, I never thought I'd drive up here again and be this happy. I have you to thank for that."

Their food arrived and they both ate carefully and quietly.

Larry's mind wasn't spinning the way it usually did when he shared a meal with someone. He thought it was probably true that all of the years eating in the University cafeteria had helped to desensitize him.

Maybe he was finally outgrowing some of his Asperger Syndrome tendencies. He looked at Sara. "I guess I should tell you Sara, and I will completely understand if, well…I have Asperger Syndrome."

Sara smiled at him. "I guessed as much, Larry. I had a feeling right away when we first started talking. I don't want you to take this the wrong way, but it is actually a relief to see you in person and know that you can tolerate a hug from me and have a meal and are looking forward to going out to the knit shop today."

Larry couldn't believe what he was hearing. How

could she possibly have known?

Sara continued, "Until we finally got the right diagnosis for Mikka, we were told he was on the autism spectrum. I immersed myself in learning about how I could help him have the best life possible. His physical symptoms were so, so extreme that I felt like there must be another explanation. I met lots of Aspies along the way, both as professionals and in his treatment groups. I have a special fondness for the community. One of the best lessons I learned from Mikka's life is that we are all on the spectrum somewhere."

Larry took a long drink of water and tried to think about what a community of Aspies might look like. He shook his head. "Wow, Sara. Nobody has ever heard that news and been glad about it. I don't really know what to think."

Sara smiled again. "Don't worry, Larry. Your brain will think about it in so many ways that I will not be able to keep up with. You can tell me about it after you have finished processing it."

The server brought their checks and swiped their room cards.

Larry jumped up to pull Sara's chair out for her. He stood very still, not sure what to do next.

Sara started to walk towards the elevator. "I thought you might need some time to work on your presentation for tomorrow, Larry. How about if we meet here around 11:30 for a quick lunch and then I will drive us to the knitting shop and we can decide on our afternoon plans."

Larry nodded happily. She really did understand his need to process all of this. "Thank you, Sara." He fished his bag out from under the table and walked toward her.

They got into the elevator together, and off at their separate floors.

Larry walked to his hotel room, opened the door and

threw his carry on bag on the bed that was neatly made already. He did the quietest jig possible so as not to disturb anyone else. This was going splendidly. Sara was right, he needed to review his notes for tomorrow and get ready for his lunch meeting with Rick.

At 11:30, Sara and Larry met for lunch. They chatted about what they might be interested in looking at in the knitting store and what it would be like at the NIH the next day. Sara had been there a number of times before and helped Larry understand what the procedure was. He made notes on his map. His biggest concern was the lunch meeting.

Sara suggested that once he was seated for the first session, he could text Rick and ask for the location of their meeting. Then he could mark it on the map, and if necessary, scope it out between sessions to be sure he knew where it was.

Larry sighed happily and folded the map carefully, a clear picture already forming in his mind.

They paid their bills for lunch and headed for the front entrance.

Larry hesitated at the revolving door.

Sara took his elbow firmly and steered him through.

A car almost exactly the same make and model of Larry's waited at the curb. It was blue instead of gray, but still very familiar.

The valet parking attendant opened the passenger door.

Larry climbed in and ran his hand over the ledge in front of him. She kept it in excellent shape. He buckled himself into the seat and put his carry on bag at his feet.

Sara got in behind the steering wheel. She patted the dash affectionately. "This car has been with me a long time, Larry. She's a good one. I call her Bessie."

Larry nodded absently. He never understood why people named their inanimate objects. "It is sort of uncanny,

Sara, but we even drive the same kind of car. Mine is gray, not blue, but they are probably close to the same year and everything. Mine is very dependable as well, but I don't name my cars."

Sara laughed as she pulled away from the curb and out into the mostly deserted street. "I know it is silly, but she feels like an old friend."

Larry didn't know what to say, so he just looked out the window, memorizing the route. He knew his brain would file it in the "Remembering the Way" folder and he'd be able to access it later.

They pulled up in front of a building and Sara leaned forward to look up out of the front windshield.

"We got really lucky, Larry, just a half a block to walk to the store."

Larry unbuckled himself and opened the car door after checking in the side view mirror to be sure nothing was approaching on the sidewalk. He climbed out awkwardly and leaned back in to retrieve his bag. He hit the back of his head on the doorframe as he was getting out.

Sara was locking the car and didn't see it happen.

He thought to himself that he had never ridden in the passenger seat of his own car and gotten out on that side where there was a high curb. He'd have to remember that. He straightened up and followed Sara to the store.

It was indeed, as the name suggested, on the second story of a building.

The shop was well lit and clean with lots of yarn and finished garments so that people could see how the yarn knit up.

Sara greeted the owner happily and gave her a hug. Larry pretended to be very busy looking at a label on some cashmere, but Sara waved for him to come over.

"This is my friend Larry, he's a knitter too."

"Welcome, Larry, we're glad to have you. Let me

know if you need help finding anything."

Larry bowed in her direction, then straightened up and said "Thank you. Such a well stocked and clean shop you have."

He was very glad that there were only a few customers in the store. Nobody seemed to be wearing any strong perfume or talking too loud. He relaxed a little and followed Sara around the shop as she picked out the yarns on her list. She seemed to really like the blue/green/purple family of colors. Larry picked up various skeins of yarn, trying to guess the fiber content before he looked at the labels. He was usually pretty good at this game. He picked out a deep grey merino, silk and cashmere blend. He carried the skein around with him to see whether he had any kind of reaction to it. He liked the weight and the softness of it.

Sara turned around to see what he was holding "Oh, Larry, that is beautiful! What are you going to make?"

Larry shrugged. "I never know what I am going to make. I guess it is like the sculpture that Michelangelo talked about. You just take away the extra bits until the form is revealed in the stone."

Sara smiled. "That's amazing, Larry. I have to follow a pattern. I understand the math behind the shapes and how to achieve them, but I don't do the calculations myself. So I guess you are unventing, like Elizabeth Zimmerman!"

Larry nodded. "Yes, exactly. That's one of the things that got me interested in the knitting. I always thought of it as purely practical, to make things to keep warm. Once I got the idea of unventing, it helped me solve a lot of problems with my work."

They walked around the store a few more times, and sat on the couch while Sara looked through the pattern books.

Larry felt his brain relax. He exhaled deeply and closed his eyes. He retraced the route they had come from the hotel and pictured the drive back. He jumped when Sara tapped him on the arm.

"You look like you are ready to get back to the hotel, Larry. Let's check out and be on our way."

Larry agreed. He was ready to go for a long run on the treadmill in the hotel gym. There had been a lot to process, and he wanted to get through it before he had to start planning for tomorrow.

Once back at the hotel, they made plans to meet for dinner at Meritage again.

Larry went off to the gym, and he guessed Sara was probably swatching with her new yarn and needles. He didn't think she seemed like the type to just cast on a project and not have a good idea how the yarn was going to behave. He dialed up the speed on the treadmill and added some extra incline. He was glad to have the gym to himself.

He often made odd noises when he was processing and he knew they bothered some people. He thought they might not bother Sara. He was still trying to figure out how she had guessed about the Asperger Syndrome from talking to him on the phone. He shook his head to clear that thought and went over their interactions so far.

He didn't find anything in the recollection that made him want to correct his behavior for the next encounter, except for the getting out of the car thing. Satisfied that it was probably going well, Larry let himself relax into a deeper more meditative state and happily ran for an hour. He could feel the endorphins rise and then slowly fade away, letting him truly relax. He did a nice long cool down, retrieved his bag from the locker and climbed the stairs back to his room.

Once inside, he checked his messages on his phone and his laptop. Nothing urgent or important. He read his notes about Rick, the session descriptions and went over the maps again. Satisfied that he had processed everything adequately, he took a shower, dressed for dinner and met Sara at the restaurant.

This time she was there first. She waved to him from the same table they had been seated at the day before. Larry could recognize her in this context. He hoped he'd get better at recognizing her in other places, the way he had been able to do with Albert and a few other people. It took intense concentration, and despite his best efforts, sometimes it didn't work.

They had a pleasant dinner and Sara showed Larry the swatch she had been working on. He was delighted to see she had attached a small tag to the end of the yarn where she wrote the needle size and the intended project she was working towards. Larry showed her the hat he had knit and Sara seemed to understand the point of knitting his thesis title into it.

Then Sara let him know that she wasn't going to be attending the Rare Disease Day with him.

Larry tried to look disappointed, but thought he understood when she said that it would be too painful for her.

She said she was happy to remain at the hotel and just knit and if Larry would like, she could drive him to the airport Tuesday morning, saving him a trip in the shuttle. It was on her way home, she said.

Larry said he would think about it, that it was a very kind offer.

She hugged him again in the elevator before they went to their rooms that night, and Larry even tried to hug her back.

He held the door open for her and said, "I guess I'll see you tomorrow evening after the conference Sara."

She nodded and waved to him when she got to her room.

He let the elevator door slide closed and breathed a

deep sigh of relief. He went through his pre-conference checklist, read the agenda again and turned in for the night.

Larry's recollection of the conference was still not quite clear. That was one of the drawbacks of his Asperger Syndrome Processing System. He could tell you quite clearly and quickly what day of the week his eleventh birthday had fallen on, and what color socks he'd worn at his High School graduation, but events like the conference with all of their layers of social and emotional interactions took much longer for Larry to fully process.

He remembered going to the NIH campus on the shuttle bus and being directed through the security process. After being fingerprinted and having his picture taken for his identification badge, he had taken detailed notes from the morning sessions and remembered feeling quite overwhelmed by the packed auditorium and his inability to sit where he would have preferred.

It was a mix of patients and their families, advocates, scientific researchers and industry professionals, so the program seemed to careen along based on the questions asked by the audience.

Larry remembered getting a text from Rick after the first session, with details of the lunch meeting place. He was relieved to find that it was a private conference room with a catered lunch. He remembered that he had walked past the cafeteria on his way to the meeting room and the lines had been long and loud with people buzzing about the presentations.

Once inside the quiet conference room, Larry had been a little lost without an agenda, only a lunch menu. Rick had greeted him and a server had come around to take their lunch order.

Rick had turned on a presentation screen and was loading his slides from his laptop while he explained to

Larry that they were just waiting for one more person to arrive and then they would begin.

Larry had taken out his notepad, and began to review his notes from the morning sessions.

A tall lanky man had burst into the room, as if he had been running to get there. He had sprinted over to Larry and held out his hand. "I've been waiting years to meet you, Larry! I'm Antti Koskinen. Sorry to be late."

Larry remembered being stunned and hoped he had responded appropriately. All he could remember now was that he had said something about having read Antti's research and being flattered by the mentions in the acknowledgements.

Antti had laughed and greeted Rick and the two other gentlemen from the Foundation. Larry could not remember their names. Antti had ordered his lunch and sat down next to Larry while Rick went through his slides.

There were timelines and milestones including clinical trials in Boston and Finland. It was a very ambitious plan that combined Antti's work with Larry's.

Antti had been working on a new way to use an older arthritis drug repurposed to help patients who were in end stage renal failure. The early research had been overwhelmingly positive, and they had patients lined up for the first clinical trials in the coming year.

Lunch had arrived, and Larry had listened to Antti excitedly describe how they intended to proceed.

After presenting slides of his own, which included a very thorough and complete understanding of Larry's work; Antti had motioned to one of the other gentleman who had passed a thick stack of paperwork across the table to Larry.

"You only need to sign the top form today, Larry. It is the standard nondisclosure form, and we'll provide you with a copy to take back to your legal team back at the

University. The rest of the paperwork is a job offer. We hope you will find it satisfactory."

Larry remembered trying to eat calmly and not choke on his food. Everything seemed to happen in fast forward motion after that. He thought he remembered giving Antti the information about how to contact Pekka, and shaking his hand, telling him he was looking forward to working with him. He also thought he remembered shaking Rick's hand, thanking him for the delicious lunch, and the other gentlemen's as well, but he couldn't be sure. He knew he had gone to the afternoon sessions, but his notes from those talks had been shaky and disconnected. Not his usual style at all.

He had texted Albert in the shuttle on the way back to the hotel. "Job offer. Will need your help."

The response was nearly immediate.

"Sure thing, pal. Congratulations!"

Larry had checked to be sure he had his bag several times and patted his pockets on the way back to the hotel, feeling like he might have forgotten something, but everything seemed to be in order.

He had texted Sara. "Lots to tell you. On the way back to the hotel now."

She had made reservations for dinner, and thought he might need time to decompress before then.

Larry was very grateful for her understanding and kindness. He had changed into his workout clothes and gone for a very long uphill run in the hotel gym.

After a shower, he'd changed into his dinner clothes and met Sara in the restaurant.

He had tried to explain the day to her, but there were so many things he hadn't processed that he felt like it was all still swirling around in his head.

She had encouraged him to just process it once he got home, as he was able to, and just enjoy the meal.

He slept fitfully that night and woke up every hour on the hour thinking it was time to check out and get on the road.

In the morning, Sara was waiting for him by the curb at exactly the time they had prearranged.

They talked mostly about knitting and the weather and remembrances of their school days on the way to the airport.

Larry pulled his carry on bag onto his lap and gripped the handle tightly.

"Sara," he said hesitantly "do you think we might be, I mean do you think it is possible that we are in love? I look forward to our phone calls and I felt completely at ease with you here in Bethesda, and I want to spend more time with you doing things like going to the grocery store and picking out new glasses. Do you think that is what it means to be in love, Sara?" Larry closed his eyes tightly and held his breath.

Sara spoke softly "Yes, Larry, I do think that it is possible. I think being in love is like swimming. Some people take to it right away and do it easily and naturally, like they just remember the way to swim. Other people are terrified of putting their faces in the water and are afraid of what else might be in the water, or if they are doing it wrong. I had sort of made up my mind that I wasn't going to swim anymore, if you know what I mean, Larry."

He nodded, happily, opening his eyes again and exhaling. "Yes, Sara. I think I know that what you mean is that swimming is a metaphor for love. I like to swim. I especially like being under water, at the bottom of the deep end, where all of the confusing noise of the world melts away and it is so calm and peaceful and I can just be myself. If that is what love is like, then I think I would like to try and take swimming lessons with you."

Sara laughed. "Oh, Larry, you are such a delight. Really, I love you!"

Larry could hardly believe what he was hearing.

He cleared his throat a couple of times and said quietly "I love you too, Sara."

He could feel his heart pounding in his temples and he gripped the handle of his carry on bag even tighter. He waited for the panic of regret to rush over him, but it never did. They rode in silence for the last mile to the airport.

When they pulled up to the curb for check-in, Larry hopped out of the car and retrieved his suitcase.

He felt as though he was underwater, looking out at all of the other travelers from a place of complete calm.

He looked at Sara and sighed. "Thank you, Sara."

Sara ran over to him at the curb, made an awkward attempt to kiss him on the cheek, and hugged him tightly.

"Safe travels, Larry. Love you!"

Larry felt a little dizzy, as if he had shot up to the surface too fast after being deep under water.

"I'll text you when I get home, Sara. Safe travels to you, too."

He opened the door for her, and she got back into her car and drove away, waving to him over her shoulder.

He stood on the curb, waving, for a long time, until a baggage agent tapped him on the shoulder. Larry jumped, startled.

"Check your bag, sir?"

Larry nodded. He found his travel documents and handed them over with his ID. "She loves me," he whispered under his breath.

"Excuse me?" said the baggage agent.

"Sara. She loves me!" said Larry incredulously.

"Oh, that's great sir, congratulations. Did you pack your bags yourself?"

Larry nodded. He collected his boarding pass and his baggage receipt. He fumbled in his pockets to retrieve his wallet and pulled out a tip for the agent as he returned his ID to the proper slot.

The rest of the trip was a complete blur to Larry. He texted Sara when he got to the shuttle bus for the ride home, and was happy to learn that she had arrived home safely and was looking forward to their next phone call.

He remembered waking up the next day, having fallen asleep still dressed in his traveling clothes, with a terrible headache.

It took him several days to get back on his regular schedule. By then he had already turned over the paperwork to Albert, who was happily negotiating the terms of his new job contract for him.

The daily phone calls with Sara kept him grounded. He thought otherwise he might not even have known what day it was.

Albert put together a package that Larry could scarcely believe.

He'd have a lab at his disposal, a room at the local Residence Inn for a year, with a car service to take him to and from the lab and all of the meetings. Two research trips a year were planned to Finland, and a companion ticket was provided.

Albert had winked at Larry. "For Sara, unless you'd rather take someone else."

Larry hadn't gotten the joke, and wondered who else he would take, but Albert got him back on track.

Albert's wife Susan knew an excellent real estate agent, and recommended a corporate moving company to pack everything except Larry's personal items and move it all to storage until Larry had decided where he wanted to live.

Larry had felt unsteady and seasick during this whole process, as if the ground was moving beneath him.

He had called his brother with the news, and Brian had

been thrilled, offering to help in any way he could.

Sara had been reassuring throughout the process and helped him set up systems and checklists, but it wasn't until he had actually arrived in Boston and checked into the Residence Inn that he really believed it was all happening.

Now here he was, in his very own lab, with patients enrolled in clinical trials, a generous salary and a retirement package.

Sara was going to come and visit this weekend.

Larry stroked his lucky vest absent mindedly as he logged in to his new computer and checked in with his team.

AFTERWARD

I hope this book serves to spark a conversation about people who are differently abled. As the parent of two adults on the autism spectrum, I prefer not to use the term disabled. For more information on person centered language and self-identity, the website for this book is:
 www.rememberingtheway.com

For more information about Autism and Asperger Syndrome, please visit The Autism Society's website http://www.autism-society.org and the ASPEN (Asperger Syndrome Education Network) Website:
http://www.aspennj.org

To learn more about kidney disease, please visit The National Kidney Foundation website:
https://www.kidney.org/kidneydisease

If you would like to discuss this book with your book club or advocacy group, here are some questions to get you started:

The story is told from Larry's perspective. How would it be different if Sara were the narrator?

Were you disappointed that the relationship between Larry and Sara was unresolved?

Do you think the relationship has a chance to move beyond the parallel play aspect of friendship?

Which character did you most strongly identify with?

Do you know somebody like Larry?

Did you learn something from the book?

If you were diagnosed with a disorder or disease, would you choose to self-identify that way?

Did the writing style convey Larry's personality?

ABOUT THE AUTHOR

Usually these are written in the third person. I'd like to change that convention. I am a spinner of stories, a writer with more than thirty years of experience as an advocate for people who are differently abled. The conventional storyline begins with a diagnostic-centered statement such as; "John is autistic. He has social anxiety and a fear of loud noises. Despite the overwhelming odds against him, he has managed to find useful, meaningful work as a website content editor." This creates an image of someone engaged in a constant battle to overcome disability. I try, whenever possible, to use person-centered language. For example, "John likes banjo music, doing crossword puzzles and playing video games. He has a photographic memory and a passion for baseball statistics. He works in the IT department of the local University. John has an autism spectrum disorder." This wording creates an image of a person with abilities. We all have different strengths and weaknesses. As the parent of two amazing and talented adults who happen to have autism spectrum disorders, I would like to encourage you to think about the ways we have been conditioned to speak about others and ourselves.

Several years ago, I decided to write a series of books featuring characters who are differently abled, using person-centered language. This is the first of the books to be published. I have several other books in the pipeline.

I enjoy spinning yarn as well as narratives, and am a life-long knitter. I have a Bachelor's Degree in Art from Guilford College with a minor in Social Justice. Growing up in the San Francisco Bay Area, I defied convention early on, racing quarter midgets at age four. My early career goals included being an outfielder for the San Francisco Giants.